TAKE A DEEP BREATH

MARE EPHRATHAH

Copyright © 2025 by Mare Ephrathah

All rights reserved. No part of this publication may be reproduced, stored or transmitted in any form or by any means, electronic, mechanical, photocopying, recording, scanning, or otherwise without written permission from the publisher. It is illegal to copy this book, post it to a website, or distribute it by any other means without permission.

This novel is entirely a work of fiction. The names, characters and incidents portrayed in it are the work of the author's imagination. Any resemblance to actual persons, living or dead, events or localities is entirely coincidental.

Mare Ephrathah has no responsibility for the persistence or accuracy of URLs for external or third-party Internet Websites referred to in this publication and does not guarantee that any content on such Websites is, or will remain, accurate or appropriate.

First edition

This book was professionally typeset on Reedsy.
Find out more at reedsy.com

*For everyone who never had a choice,
may you find the strength to use your voice.*

Preface

TRIGGER & CONTENT WARNINGS

Post-traumatic stress disorder, suicidal thoughts, abuse of a minor, sexual abuse, grooming, disassociation, and panic attacks

Look away now if you don't want to know what happens to the dog.
SPOILER AHEAD
...
I'M WARNING YOU
...

(He lives…as if I'd kill off the dog. *pfft.*)

PART ONE

IN

CHAPTER ONE

OVER THE EDGE

Faces swirled in the colorless cotton candy mist beneath me. They dared me to jump, whispering at me to trust in vapor. The bottom was nowhere to be seen. I imagined stepping onto the fog as if it would carry me away. For a moment, I entertained the thought. *What if I don't fall?* But the fantasy ripped apart as reality flashed in bright vivid pulses of red and twisted limbs.

I swallowed back my saliva and retreated a few feet before sitting down. My hands trembled as I rubbed them together and with a sigh, I closed my eyes and concentrated on my surroundings. The rock underneath me was firm, wet, but firm.

Inhale...exhale...the air is cold.
Inhale...exhale...my legs are on fire.
Breathe.
Clear your mind. Darkness swirled around me.
Dark. Nothing. I am nothing.
Inhale; cold fingers wrapped around my thighs.
Exhale; cinnamon. I shifted and scrunched up my nose.
Empty your mind. Ashen palms entered my vision and

grasped my throat.

Stop!

Everything vanished. A valley of pines appeared before me, jutting through the top of the fog. Warmth spread over my face and I smiled as the sky shifted from navy to pink. Time stopped. Peace flowed through my pores and encircled my heart. I could only ever dream of a sight like this. Part of me didn't want to accept that any of it was real. Another part of me knew deep down that it wouldn't last. My face twisted.

Why couldn't I block them out?

"So much for meditation," I muttered to the void. Even out here, where they couldn't touch me, I had no escape. My mind was forever a prison to the haunting memories. My stomach turned, but the usual quickening of saliva didn't follow. At least I'd made some progress. *You should see a therapist,* I thought and instantly snorted. They were another manipulator in disguise. I could *never* see a therapist. Even when the chatter in my mind – all the words I could never voice, tightly bottled inside – became a clamoring noise that refused to simmer.

A rustling behind me cut through my mind's chatter and now silence was all I could hear. I thought it might've been my dog, but *that* was no husky. Staring straight through me was the biggest damn bear I'd ever seen in my life. My chest seized and my stomach fell to the chasm behind me. *Where was Wolf?*

My heart remembered it was supposed to beat and went into hyperdrive. My legs shook as I struggled to stand, inching up with as little movement as I could muster. I clenched my jaw trying to summon what on earth I was supposed to do. *Should I run?* I wondered as I sought out an escape. My mind grasped for straws, panic settling into the recesses of my veins.

Inhale; the bear took a step.

Exhale; I reached for the gun at my waist.

Its claws could easily gore through my organs in one quick swipe; I had no time. I clicked back the hammer. There were worse things than death. My body winced at the vicious bark to my right. *Wolf.* The bear lobbed its head towards his growling shriek. The bear's lips curled, revealing thick fang-like teeth. A rumble tore from it's belly and Wolf bounded forward, snapping at it's heels.

The bear lunged for him and before I could blink, my finger clasped around the trigger. Smoke flashed and my eardrums burst—and so did my hopes. The bear's shoulder muscle flinched at the impact, brushing it off like a horse to a fly. Then it turned it's head my way. It's pupils widened. All 500 pounds now bounded toward me. I snapped my head to the valley behind, my feet backed to the precipice. Flashes of Wolf's gray fur bounced behind the bear, but he couldn't save me. My heart felt like it was going to vibrate out of my chest. My hands shook too violently to steady the gun.

Four feet away.

Three.

Two. I held my breath.

Right before it reached me, right before its teeth sank into my neck, the bear's back feet slid on an unstable slab. Her momentum launched her forwards, barreling across the empty space between us. I fell to the ground as the massive brown body hurled past, inches away from its intended target. Its thick stench followed as rocks flew everywhere. I grunted when dirt and gravel whipped into my eyes. The bear roared and flailed over the edge. A searing pain scathed my ankle as its claw pulled me down the side of the cliff.

I screamed and flailed for a hold. *Please God, don't let me die.*

My fingers grasped a clod of moss, only to tear it from the stone. My forearms burned while I found and held onto a tiny nook with everything I had. Sickening thumps sounded from below as the bear bounced off each boulder to the bottom.

Wolf's wet nose ran along my forearm. Without thinking about it, I grasped onto his front legs. At a nod of my head, he took a step back, and then another. My hips scraped along the edge of the rock and I yanked a leg up. Able to get on both knees, I crawled away from the precipice. Both of our chests heaved frantically. My stomach turned, bile formed in my mouth. My abs clenched as coffee heaved out of my body. With a shaky hand I wiped my mouth and turned around.

What on earth just happened? My legs were still wobbling as I attempted to stand and peer over the edge. My knees felt weak. Heights didn't typically scare me but I contemplated never climbing again. The fog hadn't dissipated. I couldn't see below it, couldn't see if the bear was down there. Alive or dead. It would have to be some kind of supernatural being to survive that fall. I backed away. Wolf's warm body pressed against my thigh. Blotches of scarlet smeared along the side of his body, causing me to sharply inhale.

"Buddy!" I cried. I crouched down to examine him, but I couldn't find a cut.

That's when I remembered the pain in my ankle. The searing pain that I'd somehow forgotten. Suddenly, it hurt to stand. I clenched my jaw and felt sick again. There was a nice long gouge from the back of my calf, wrapping around under my ankle. *That's not good.* I was lucky the bear had just grazed me, lucky it didn't drag me off the cliff with it. However, a wound like this in the wilderness could kill me if I wasn't careful. I still had the hike down and didn't have anything on hand to clean it with. I tried to locate my water bottle. I could at least rinse my gash until I could properly cleanse it. I almost spun myself dizzy trying to find it, but the bottle was gone — likely laying at the bottom beside the monstrous beast that almost took my life. My body felt like it might fall out from under me

I chuckled and pushed back my hair. Wolf cocked his head to the side, peering at me like I was a little too delirious even given the circumstances. Perhaps I was. But one moment I was on a high from the hike, quieting my thoughts, and the next I was facing a bear and certain death. My mind reeled as it replayed the last few minutes. I didn't know what to think or feel; confusion perhaps was the best sum of where I was, laced with adrenaline. What I knew for certain was that we needed to make it back to the bottom. And hopefully not run into another bear.

A second laugh escaped my lips. I thought I'd find some solace in nature where man rarely went. Nope. Even nature wanted to hurt me.

"Why?!" I yelled towards the sky as if I might receive an answer. I stared and waited, but no answer ever came. I didn't know why I bothered. No one ever cared about me, not really. Why would God be any different?

Wolf pushed his nose into my palm, reminding me that he cared. He always had, but he was a dog. I plopped down and leaned into his soft fur, burying my face into his shoulder. Part of me wished I'd fallen instead of the bear. If not for Wolf, I don't think I would have fought at all.

"Why do men say they are like dogs? They are *nothing* like dogs," I whispered to Wolf.

I took a shaky inhale and forced my wobbly legs to stand. Hiking back down a mountain now made me want to hurl. At least it was all downhill. My first step forward was met with a sharp stab to my ankle. I scanned the area, but I didn't see anything I could use as a walking stick. Had I been a smarter hiker, I would have had one already. I didn't want the extra gear—which also meant the lack of a pack where I would have some first aid. All because it was supposed to be a simple morning walk up the mountain. I balled my fists and hobbled towards the tree line. Surely there would be branches in there.

"Yes!" I exclaimed after a couple minutes of surveying the forest floor. There were several to choose from. As I bent down to pick one up, something rustled deep in the dark of the forest. I froze but Wolf seemed unbothered.

"Come on," I whispered and nodded Wolf back to the path. It was probably just a rabbit…or a bird. I couldn't shake the uncanny feeling that I was being watched. Eyes drilled into me as I nearly skidded across the dirt down the mountain. I smelled cinnamon again and a black figure flashed in my peripheral. I bit my lip to keep from crying.

Wolf was calm, trotting by my side, absolutely unaffected by the fear in me. Every few seconds his body would nudge into me. He may not share my fear, but he could sense the panic setting in. I needed to gain control. I was imagining things. We still had that one section of the path to get through that always set me on edge. The hair on the back of my neck stood up thinking about it.

The forest narrowed in and the morning sun could barely penetrate through the leaves, making an almost unnatural darkness for the time of day. It took three minutes to get through. I knew because I timed it. Chills prickled along my forearm. I paused, knowing what was ahead, and scanned the forest around me before I was suffocated by it. Everything was calm. Morning birds chirped to the upbeat tempo of their cheery hearts.

"Everything's fine. Just fine. I'm fine." I said, not sounding fine at all. I gripped my stick and trudged forward. No one else was in the forest. There were no eyes watching my every step. Nothing was going to jump out at me.

"One, two, three, four..." I counted my way through, focusing on the numbers instead of the cool darkness closing in around me or the fog bobbing above my head. I didn't allow my mind to wander to the fact that I'd smelled cinnamon earlier, or that I'd seen a shadow weave through the narrow trunks.

"One hundred twenty-five, one hundred twenty six—"

The light of the morning sun in the distance beamed reality into my heart. After a few more minutes I saw my van. Wolf ran to it, knowing it meant breakfast, leaving me alone for the rest of the path. My van was the only vehicle. There was almost always at least one other hiker or nature lover out here. Even if it was sickly early.

I didn't waste too much time thinking about it and grabbed the first aid from under my makeshift sink in the side of my van and cleaned up the wound. The gash looked large enough to need stitches. Something I didn't have the knowledge or equipment to take care of. I shoved the thought of a hospital away and covered the slit with gauze. I could google it later.

As I shut the side door and hopped into the driver's seat, I realized I hadn't even looked for the bear. I couldn't see the body out of the windshield. Where it had landed I wasn't sure and I wasn't about to take more time out here hobbling around like wounded prey looking for it.

When I drove out of the park, I decided to make a quick stop at the ranger station. Jerry needed to know about the bear.

But when I got there, his truck wasn't in sight. *Maybe he parked around the side?* The clock on my dash told me it was too early. He probably wasn't here yet. But I had to try.

The sound of my van door shutting echoed loud enough to alert anyone. Gravel crunched under my boots. A light breeze wrapped around my neck and caused me to shiver. The station was a small beige shed with a glass window. Plain and practical. I knocked on the door and waited. After a few minutes of silence, I peered inside only to find it empty. I had two choices. Forget about it or —

CHAPTER TWO

BRIDGET

I let out an interminable sigh. No response. The worn mahogany desk echoed off my chipped nails as I tapped them in rhythm over the smooth surface. Still, he refused to look up from his piece of paper. He wasn't actually reading it. A deep crease formed at the edge of his left eyebrow. I probably deserved the treatment honestly, but I couldn't help feeling agitated.

"Sheriff Rosen!" I yelled with a clenched fist. He replicated my sigh and shook his paper. It crumpled as I snatched it out of his hands.

"What do you want, Jay?" He looked up, holding back a stupid smirk that made me want to sock him. He knew it too, all the while, secretly glad to see me. Even if he was still pissed. It didn't matter much though.

"I was attacked by a bear," I stated. He scoffed and tilted his head.

"Were you now? Isn't this something you should be reporting to the park ranger?"

I pursed my lips, "You know, I would have, if someone was there. Unfortunately, you were the next best option."

"What do you want me to do about it?" he asked, still

leaning in his swivel chair, hands clasped over his protruding chest. Had I been anyone else, he would have jumped with concern. The cork board behind him stared back at me with haunting black and white faces. *Was my face plastered on a board somewhere?* I imagined the families that were heart broken and torn about loved ones gone missing.

My family didn't miss me. If I was on a board, it wouldn't be for the same reason.

"I don't know," I said, "but if someone happens upon a bear with a bullet wound at the bottom of Crier Ridge, you know why. If it's not there and it somehow managed to survive and goes and kills someone, at least I did my part!" I flung my hands in the air. He stood up so fast he could've knocked himself out. His ridiculous grin vanished and he cleared his throat. His bulging eyes traced along my bandaged leg.

"You weren't joking. Are you okay? I thought you were trying to get a rise out of me. You know, this is exactly why you should carry a phone!" He was scolding me…again, like a child. It was my life, my business, and the sheriff needed to learn how to butt out.

"I'm fine," I said, looking down. And that's when I noticed it. The paper I'd snatched from him had a handwritten note on it. Dashed in chicken scratch was a name that sent my heart into my stomach. My breath seized in my chest and my vision turned to fog. I had to reach for the desk to keep from collapsing.

This couldn't be real. I had to be hallucinating.

"You're sure you're okay?" he asked, trying to grab me, but I reeled back. I shook my head. This couldn't be. It just couldn't. I wanted to cry and scream and run. I had to run.

"I have to go." I faltered backwards and turned, nearly

tripping over my feet. My face burned with fire as I pushed through the glass doors of the sheriff's station. I heard Rosen call for me, but it felt muffled and far off. The sound of my heartbeat pulsing in my head overshadowed every other noise.

I staggered into the front seat of my van and yanked the door shut behind me. My legs locked up like steel and my chest felt as if it might combust. The fire slithered into my neck. I clenched my eyes and gripped the leather steering wheel. Wolf's wet nose was on my face in an instant. Before I could blink, he was in my lap. I focused on my breath as his weight sunk into me.

Inhale...exhale. Breathe. Breathe. Fucking breathe Jay. The grip on my heart crumbled like a sand castle and the pain crawling up my neck softened. I slid my shaking hand from the wheel and slumped forward into Wolf. I didn't know how long I sat there. When I opened my eyes, the world was a shade of ochre. A scream forced itself from my body at the sudden tapping to my left. Wolf growled at the figure.

"Good boy," I whispered before clicking my fingers towards the back seat. Wolf jumped behind me with ease but turned around and shoved his head next to my shoulder. The breeze hissed into the van as I rolled down the window. Sheriff Rosen stood there with a scowl on his face and a hand on the side of the door as he stooped forward.

"How long have you been standing there?" I asked through gritted teeth.

"Long enough to know you need help," he said. I rolled my eyes. I didn't need any help.

"Jay," he reached for my hand but I pulled away, "Why don't you let people help you? They might surprise you."

"That's exactly what I'm afraid of," I said. I was done trusting people. They always betrayed you. Rosen flicked his finger towards my hand. I looked down. My fist was still locked onto the slip of paper I'd taken from him.

"You know something about that?" he asked. I shook my head and handed it back. Truth was, I did. I knew exactly who Bridget Cummings was. What I didn't know was why that name was on that paper. Here. In this town. The only possible answer was - they found me.

"Listen," Sheriff Rosen took a large inhale, "I don't know what happened to make you so cynical and I'm done trying to figure it out. I'm gonna do this one last thing, because I know you're lying." Meeting his gaze, I swallowed hard and grit my teeth.

"A guy came in here about twenty minutes ago, looking for a girl with that name."

"You can't just give out that kind of information!" I blurted. He tilted his head with raised eyebrows.

"No. No, I can't, even if I knew who this person was." He waved the crumpled paper.

"Right, which you don't."

"I didn't." he said, eyebrows raised.

"You didn't? As in past tense?" My breath came in more rapidly and I tried to bite it down.

"I was waiting on a report for that name in my system, when you came in." he said and my head started to spin.

He looked down for a heartbeat and then up. "What are you running from?"

Oh my god, he knew. I mean it couldn't be that hard for a cop, I guess. Find a missing persons report, it probably had a picture. Dig deeper, find the name change.

"My past," was all I could get out. It felt as if my throat was going to close up. Hope drained from his face. He knew I wasn't going to let him in. I didn't let anyone in, and the fact that he felt he should be privileged to that just pissed me off even more.

"Well, you should probably go then." He backed away from me. I saw the wound in his eyes. I wanted to care. But I couldn't. He should have left me alone. He should have known I was a lost cause.

"Bye, Brett," I uttered his name for the last time and put the van in drive.

CHAPTER THREE

A LIGHT IN THE DARK

I had no idea where I was going, but I knew I couldn't stay. My hands tightened around the steering wheel and I glanced in the rear view mirror at Wolf, who lay entirely oblivious on the mattress in the back. I'd hoped with everything I had that it wasn't too late. I bit back the sting in my eyes as I considered what might happen to him if they caught me. He was all I had...but more than that, I was all *he* had. But for right now, in this moment—this single moment in time—I was safe. It was only Wolf and I here. Just the two of us. No one threatening me. No one to take my body and use it as they pleased.

I grimaced as I remembered the warm bodies against mine. I felt their skin sticking to me as if it wasn't a memory. Like it wasn't more than five years ago. Like they were something I could never wash off. I shifted in my seat, smelling their scent, their whispers crawling through my ears. I tried to block it out. Despite my efforts, it crashed in waves to the front of my mind.

The road before me dissipated, replaced by a small, barely lit room with a light aroma of vanilla and cinnamon. My skin crawled. Hair shoved into my nose as I gagged, unable to breathe. That was the last I remembered of that night. It was all too much for a little girl. But nobody cared. Nobody gave a damn; and nobody believed the next Sunday, in church, that their beloved preacher could be so vile. Instead, *I* was punished for making up stories. *I* was labeled the liar.

I forced myself to inhale and violently shook the fog in my mind. The road and its white and yellow lines stretched out in front of me. Headlights flashed in my mirror.

"What the…" *How was it dark already?* The idea that I had been stuck in my head for enough time for the sun to completely vanish sent waves of guilt and fear through me. I dug my nails into the steering wheel. I needed to pull over for the night. Far off in the distance, some gas stations and a couple fast food joints glowed a beaming welcome. Seemed as good a stop as any. No doubt Wolf had to pee.

"Hold tight, Bud," I said after parking. Wolf popped his head up as I squeezed behind the front seat. I began lightly bouncing on my toes, my own urge to pee stronger now that I was standing. I grabbed the revolver from the high shelf above my bed where it sat safely next to a worn copy of *Little House on the Prairie*.

When your childhood is a nightmare, you hold on to the slivers of anything good, anything whole, in an attempt to pretend you aren't in the nightmare. With a frown, I slid the gun into the holster in my pants and slipped a large brown hoodie over my head.

I had two choices. One, leave Wolf to guard the van and everything I owned in this world. Or two, take him with me into the gas station bathroom for my own protection. I glanced up. There were people in there. It wasn't that late, barely past six. But even a crowded room meant nothing. People were blind or worse, cowards. I sighed.

"In," I said after letting him go pee first, and closed the side door behind him. I'd rather be taken advantage of, possibly even murdered, then lose everything and have to sleep in the cold again. Homelessness is not for the faint of heart. My head swiveled on my shoulders as I surveyed my surroundings. Sheriff Rosen was right about me being cynical, but I had my reasons.

I made my way inside, clenching my teeth against the pain that came with each right step. There were four people in the convenience store, and I looked each of them in the eyes. People usually looked away. It made them nervous, like they were caught. I used to be that way too, but keeping my head down was too dangerous. A predator would back down from a fight. They wanted something easy. I wasn't going to give them that. Just because none of these people were specifically after Bridget, didn't mean they weren't looking for some young girl to rape.

On my way back out, I threw a gallon of water, a burrito, and a few packages of beef jerky on the counter. I could see my van through the window. Wolf sat tall and proud in the passenger seat. Putting my wallet back into my jeans, I noticed an idle car far off in the shadows. I tilted my head. I couldn't make out if anyone was inside. My heart ticked up.

"You too," I muttered back to the lady who told me to have a good night. I kept my eyes pinned on the car as I made my way to my van. It seemed to be a dark green, though it was hard to be sure. It felt out of place, sitting there in the dirt instead of the lot. Maybe it belonged to the woman at the register.

Right before I got to my door, a small square light blinked

on in the dark of the front seat of the green car. Someone *was* in there. I ducked into my van and bit the inside of my lip as the glow flashed off. I waited a minute and watched people come and go, but the car didn't leave. My palms started to sweat as I moved into the back and pulled out my laptop.

A phone would've been easier, but I was so used to not having one that I didn't mind the few minutes it took for my laptop to get going. Except tonight. Tonight my patience flitted out of my tapping fingers. I could barely see out the back window through the dusty brown curtains as I waited for something to change. Waited for the car to leave—or for a shadow to stalk my way. Taking a quick moment to peel my eyes away from the vehicle, I pulled up Google Maps and typed in Walmart. When I looked up again, the car was gone, and I exhaled.

If it weren't for the situation I was in, I'd think I was crazy. Yet, someone *was* looking for me. There was no question about that. Did I leave fast enough? Were they following me? It seemed ridiculous that they could be, but my gut screamed that it was true. Reality blared that I could *never* be careful enough. I could never stop checking enough. And I'd never be able to stop running. I thought I was safe before, hidden in the tiny rural Montana town, surrounded by its vast mountain landscape. I shook my head and climbed back into the driver's seat. Safety was an illusion. I scanned again for the green car, but it was truly gone.

I waved to another van holding up for the night in the Walmart parking lot. Van life wasn't glamorous. Truth be told, it wasn't my preference, but it was my only security, giving me the ability to run in an instant, like now. I slid the blackout covers over all the windows and double checked the locks. Then, after laying in bed for what felt like ten minutes, I checked the locks again.

The metal door was cold against my forehead, an ominous prelude to the death of winter. I hated winter. But like all horrible things in life, you can't fight it. You can only hope you make it through and come up for air when it's over.

I took a step back to the bed. My ankle was throbbing. I hadn't checked it since this morning when I first bandaged it. Not that I had a moment to between running out of town and blanking out on the drive—which sent shivers down my spine. How hadn't I caused an accident in those lost *hours*? And how did I lose hours of my day? It just couldn't be possible. Yet, it happened.

I gritted my teeth and reached for the first aid kit and bottle of peroxide under my sink. It was miraculously not out of date. I'd stocked up as soon as I got the van but never had to use any of it. I took a sharp inhale as I peeled back the bandage. It wasn't bleeding anymore. Was it swollen? I bit my lip and poked around it, terrified of seeing pus.

I let out a sigh of relief when none oozed out. It felt like being ripped open all over again as I poured the peroxide over the cut. I gripped the blanket as Wolf stared at me with his head cocked. I'd laugh if I wasn't being tormented with enough pain to steal my voice from me. Whatever would I do without him?

My fingers fumbled, tying the clean bandage over my ankle.

An intense beating in my chest threatened my steady hand and heat rose in my face. Before I could smell vanilla or cinnamon, I clamped my teeth down on the inside of my cheek. The pain stuffed the rising memory back down to the depths of my mind where it belonged. What triggered it this time, I wasn't sure, but they were more frequent than ever. Being on the run from my unknown pursuer didn't help matters.

I hadn't removed my gun from my holster and as I lay back down, its weight was a reminder of the hole I was in. With eyes closed, I focused on my breath. My jaw felt sore. It popped as I moved it back and forth and I realized I'd probably been clenching it all day.

Wolf shifted before laying his face on my stomach. He was warm and solid, the only sure thing in my whole life. I ran my fingers through his thick fur and he made a happy little moan that only huskies can do. My heart slowed and steadied. Our chests moved in unison. For just a moment, every fear vanished and I felt whole.

The sound of teenagers laughing echoed in the distance. As skateboard wheels on a hard surface rolled past, I imagined what the kids looked like. Long loose flannel shirts and jeans that constricted their calves. How people skated in such restrictive clothing, I could never understand. I heard a crash and someone's car horn going off. Laughter erupted again. I wanted to be pissed at their careless behavior. But I found myself envious of their laughter, of their happiness. Of a friendship. *Friends are only in fairy tales*, I reminded myself. Wolf shifted his head.

"It's okay," I told myself, "I have you."

CHAPTER FOUR
THE SHADOW

A hand pounding on the metal door jolted me awake. Yellow light beams broke through the edges of the curtains. I sat up and moved the black fabric back, wincing as daggers of sunlight annihilated my pupils. A man in uniform stood outside my van. *What now?* I wondered. Not wanting to open my side door - not wanting to get out at all - I moved to the front and rolled down the window.

"Hi," I said as I leaned out the window. I braved a smile, hoping to get through whatever this was quickly.

"Good morning, ma'am," he said and sauntered over. My skin crawled with each sticky step. I rubbed my stomach, hoping to calm it. I'd wished now more than ever that I'd asked Sheriff Rosen what the guy asking for me looked like. I clenched my teeth together. *Stupid, stupid, stupid.*

"I don't mean to bother you," he started and I held my breath, "You're allowed to park your vehicle here overnight, however, your tags are out of date."

"Oh. Uh." I stammered, a little relieved.

"Do you have your license and registration?" he asked. I nodded, unable to say anything yet and scrambled for the items. He looked them over and handed them back.

"I'd give you a ticket, but seeing as you're already going to be paying late fees, let's call this a warning."

I wiped my hair off my cheek, "Thank you. Yeah, I'll do that." Truth was, I had the tags, I just forgot to actually put them on. You'd think his system would bring that up. He nodded and waved before walking back to his cruiser. I leaned back into my seat and breathed a sigh of relief. Not wanting to draw more attention to myself, I rifled through the glove box for those tags.

Why didn't I take care of it right away? I tried to remember as I pressed them into my license plate. The memory felt far off. I could see myself in the post office opening it and walking back to my van. Something stopped me. My head hurt from trying to remember. I looked around me before flicking open my pocket knife and slashing Xs all through the tags.

The Sheriff's face flooded my vision. He was there that day too, flirting with the post office lady and smirking at me. My stomach churned. The sound of a stream of water hitting something and spraying shook me out of the memory. Still on my knees, I leaned to the side, peering around the van to see Wolf peeing on the front tire.

"Dude," I said. He paused, leg still hoisted in the air. I laughed and rose to my feet. I glanced behind me before opening the side door again. A breeze graced the back of my neck. I tugged my beanie down and swooped the scraggly loose bits of hair back under it. My fingers still ice, I rubbed them together and grabbed Wolf's dish bowl. He ate as I leaned against the van, surveying the half empty parking lot.

What was I going to do? *Get as far away from Seattle as possible*! I thought. *But then what? He found me in Montana. Am*

I just going to delay the inevitable a few more years? Or a few more seconds, I thought, spotting the little green Toyota from last night.

"GET in!" I yelled at Wolf and jumped in behind him before slamming the sliding door shut. I paused as my vision fought against me, a darkness encompassing everything. The world started to spin and blur and I had to grab the seat pocket to steady myself. I shook the darkness away. My head felt like a bowling ball balancing on my shoulders as I climbed into the front seat.

The car was still there. But I couldn't see anyone inside. Again. I cranked the key and the engine roared to life. When I pressed on the gas, nothing happened. Agitation rose in me as I grit my teeth and tried to find an answer. I looked down and screamed about five expletives before thrusting the gearshift out of park.

My eyes kept fluttering to my mirrors, watching for the toyota. Waiting for it to be behind me. I pulled onto the freeway but still, there was no sign of the hunter green car - though I very much still felt like I was being hunted. After twenty minutes, I wiped my wet palms over my jeans. A hint of iron seeped over my tongue. Blood. Looking into the rearview mirror at myself instead of my invisible pursuer, it was clear I'd been biting my lip this whole time. *Great*. It's amazing the damage you can inflict on yourself without ever feeling it.

Well, I was feeling it now.

My mind raced as I drove, the speedometer creeping over the limit. Again I wiped my palms, which seemed to be perpetually wet. For now, I'd just keep driving. The only vehicle behind me was a white box van. Which was ironically relieving. Pulling my side braid over my shoulder, I realized I'd panicked for no reason. There was no way someone could still be following me. No way for them to locate me. It's not like I had a tracking device. My heart picked up. I laughed. *No, I mean, come on. That's crazy. They're not that advanced now.* I drove fifty more miles in unease. The thought of someone putting a tracking device on my vehicle in the middle of the night haunted me until I found myself merging over and taking the next exit.

Wolf made a moan as he stretched in the back. While I put gas in the tank, I opened up the maps and searched for a campsite. We weren't near any Walmarts. Nothing but barren and brown leaf trees for miles. It was a ten-minute drive to the nearest site. Yet it felt like an hour. I snacked on a protein bar as we pulled in. No one was in the little box stand with glass windows. I grabbed an envelope and put in the cash before slipping it into the lock box. Didn't need someone knocking on my van in the morning again.

Wolf's nails clicked against the floor as I drove around the bend, parking the van. With the air temperature dropping with the setting sun, I grabbed my coat and hopped out. Would I really find a tracking device? Why not just wait for me to get up in the morning? Why put one there? Insurance, maybe.

I crouched down, having to lean on my un-maimed leg, but couldn't get a good look at the underside of the vehicle. What was I even supposed to be looking for? The asphalt grazed some of the skin on my back as I pushed myself under the van. I didn't see anything out of the ordinary. No blinking lights. No out of place contraptions. If it was there, it wasn't like in the movies.

I closed my eyes. Gasoline and rubber filled my senses. Dead leaves rolled by in the breeze. Wolf's heavy panting echoed in the distance. Nothing sounded out of the ordinary. Cars blew by on the highway less than a mile off. Rocks pressed into the asphalt and flicked away. Another car was pulling in. Slow. I opened my eyes. For a split second I thought it was the green Toyota but as it passed out of the sun, I realized it was black. Did that matter? What if it was never green? Maybe it had been black this whole time, or what if he changed vehicles after being spotted? I pulled my hand across my forehead. Spotted, sure. I wasn't even confident that's who was after me.

I was about to shimmy out from under the van when the car turned down my way and crept up beside me. *Great.* Not someone to take me back, just an ax murderer or thief. Wolf bounded out from the woods, his voice thundering through the trees. The car kept going. All the way around and back out, driving in the opposite direction. I let out a sigh of relief. Again. Just someone who needed to turn around. I scooched myself out and gave Wolf a happy rub down. He was gonna eat well tonight. I would make sure of that. Maybe I had a fighting chance.

I pulled all the ingredients and cooking utensils out to the weather worn, gray wood bench. The van felt too claustrophobic tonight, its walls inching in on me, pressing out all the oxygen. As I sliced my potato, oil sizzling in the little pan, a chill ran down my spine. I looked up. Just a darkening forest. But from the depths of it, I could swear someone was watching me. I could swear if I looked hard enough, a silhouette would appear in between the ghastly trunks. But Wolf lay absolutely unamused at my feet. *I'm going crazy,* I thought. If someone was lurking in the forest, Wolf would know long before I did. And when a squirrel bounded between trees, causing a branch to break, I jumped.

That's when I lost it. My mouth turned down and my body

heaved. I sat down at the bench and buried my face in my palms. The tears pushed past my clenched eyes. My shoulders convulsed and I suddenly couldn't grasp a full breath of air without wheezing. Wolf came up between my legs and nudged his muzzle onto my thigh. Sniffling and wiping my face, I caressed the top of his head. He moved back and jumped up onto the bench where I was sitting.

"Awe, Bud," I said as he lowered onto my lap. My throat felt like someone had been strangling me. My hands traced along my trachea like an eraser. But the grasp lingered. And I did my best to ignore it. My head ached with the beginning of what felt like a migraine. I closed my eyes and tried to focus on the noises around me. I found the sound of my soft beating heart. The low hum of a mumble sounded out of Wolf - a sort of lullaby. A branch shuttered and more leaves fell to the ground. I looked up, entirely relaxed now, but then began to sob again when I saw it.

A blue jay.

CHAPTER FIVE

ESCAPE

They say childhood introduces children to the wounds of the world. The way I saw it, the world must be on its last dying breath. It was my 18th birthday. The worst day of my life. And the best. I was not a child with loving parents. I was a product of two people who saw it as their right to sell. Again and again and again. I couldn't remember a lot of it, yet so much haunted me. The memories were like ghosts that fluttered at the forefront of my mind. Unpredictable was their presence.

It's scary what can become normal. It wasn't as if I was locked away in a cupboard or tied to a bed in a dark basement. I lived like every other girl my age. I went to school. I attended church on Sundays. I even had a membership at our local rock climbing gym. In between the men and women that would pay for me, I lived content - happy even - with two parents that told me they loved me. People I laughed with. People I confided in. People I trusted.

I ask myself all the time why I stayed so long. Why didn't I run away sooner? Their love was a lie I ate, like rabbit meat which satisfies the stomach but eats away the body. The term was coined as rabbit starvation. *Don't eat only rabbits if you get lost up in those mountains,* Jerry the Park Ranger had warned, *too much protein, not enough fat and carbs.* I was starving on too much affection.

One time, I fought back and wounded the man who insisted on pushing while I screamed at the tearing pain from behind. He covered my mouth and nose as I thrashed. Unable to breathe, I bit his hand, pulled away, and kneed him in his uncovered groin. It wasn't what I was supposed to do. It wasn't what he had paid for. He cracked his knuckles against my jaw and I fell to the ground. His fist pounded into me, *one, two, three.* If I remembered hard enough, I could still feel the numbing spots where he hit. Like an unseen tattoo. Pain radiated through my body as I gasped for air. My parents charged in, guns pointed at him, protecting their product…not their 12 year old daughter.

That night, as I sat at our little yellow kitchen table holding an ice pack to my face, my mother sat beside me, hand on my leg, and warned me that if I ever pulled a stunt like that again, she'd yank me out of rock climbing. I stared at her. The lines on her face were still like a map in my head. Rock climbing was my only escape. My only place of happiness. My only moment where none of this madness existed. And she knew it.

So, I didn't fight.

But then I approached my 18th birthday. It felt like the clamps were releasing. I could legally go. They didn't own me. They couldn't keep me. And most of the people who paid wanted someone younger anyways. I was finally old enough to legally have sex, yet found myself relieved that was far less likely now.

My birthday was in February and the Seattle Seahawks were in the Superbowl. We had tickets. Naively, I thought we were going to be a real family now. That I'd paid my dues. I worked for my freedom. I never saw it coming.

"Let's get drinks and dogs before we sit." Dad smiled as we entered the stands. I smiled back, barely able to contain my excitement. Mom wrapped her arm into mine as we ascended the steps.

"What do you want, honey?" her voice glimmered. I leaned my head on her shoulder and whispered the only truth I knew.

"The only condiment that belongs on hot dogs is mustard."

She chuckled and rolled her eyes, "I disagree and you should watch something other than Clint Eastwood or Little House on the Prairie."

"I highly doubt I could ever commit such a crime," I said.

"Mustard?!" dad asked, yelling over the loud bustle of conversation swooping around us. I nodded my head with wide eyes that screamed, *of course*. A couple short moments later, he was turning to us, hands full of drinks and white square boxes that held our steaming dogs. Mom and I each grabbed our orders from him before they tumbled out and crashed to the concrete.

"Where's our seats?" Mom asked dad. He handed her the tickets with the numbers and she nodded back. There was a weird look in her eyes. I almost asked her about it but two kids squished up against me as they ran past and nearly knocked my food out of my hands.

"Yikes, close one. We better make our way to our seats." Dad laughed.

At halftime, the usual trance by the latest pop star began. I didn't know who they were and I didn't care. I preferred classic rock and wished someone like The Heartbreakers were performing. I bent down to reach for my smartphone out of my purse but the man sitting next to me took hold of my wrist. I shrieked in surprise. His grip was tight and his eyes were like black holes piercing into my soul. His hair was blonde like mine, but his strength was far greater. I tried yanking away only to feel an odd popping sensation followed by a sharp stabbing pain. Panic swelled up to my throat. I swiveled my head to my dad on the other side of me as I screamed for help, but he refused to look my way.

"The money?" was all he said. I tilted my head in confusion. The blonde stranger, who couldn't be but a few years older than me, kicked a small black duffle bag across the floor, knocking over a half filled soda into my purse. Dad grunted as he bent forward to pick up the larger bag. My mouth hung open as he peeked inside and nodded.

"No..." I whispered as tears trickled out of my eyes. I knew exactly what was happening but I didn't want to believe it. My parents weren't the most moral there were, but this? *No, they wouldn't.* My heart became a counterweight inside my body and I couldn't move. The side of my dad's clean shaven face, void of emotion, burned into my brain. The stranger yanked me out of my seat and pulled me close into him. Cold hard metal dug into my rib cage. A gun.

"Dad? Mom?!" I screamed. They still refused to look at me. And no one in the audience with us seemed to notice what was happening. I searched their faces for help, but they kept trying to peer around me to see the show. Why was no one helping? Why couldn't anyone see what was happening?

"Shut up and you won't have any holes in you." He growled into my ear and twisted my already painful wrist. My lip quivered as more tears fell down my cheeks. To escape meant death. If I even could. This brute of a man was holding me into his bulky body with ease. As we exited the stadium, a cold breeze grazed my face and the fullness of what just took place hit me. A knife had been struck straight through my heart and into my spine. My knees began to buckle under the weight of a body that didn't feel like my own.

"Get up," he said, hoisting me into a vertical position. The world buzzed in and out of focus. *My parents have sold me.* They sold me one last time. Sold me to God knows who. Someone who would force drugs into my system. Threaten and blackmail me into porn. Or worse, much much worse. I didn't know. I didn't want to find out. I'd rather him shoot me right there. Die before the last ounce of dignity was bled out. I couldn't do this anymore. My entire body went limp and I sank to the sidewalk like I was a part of it. But the man didn't shoot me. He didn't hit me. He didn't inject some kind of drug. He picked me up and slung me over his shoulder.

Of course he wouldn't shoot me. Not after all that he just paid. And not with security guards still in view. So, I started screaming and thrashing, hoping to gain someone's attention. But I watched as people swerved out of our way to avoid us. I pounded my fists against the back of his head and then felt a long stab in my hamstring. Fire bursted in my leg, causing a guttural scream to echo from my lips. My leg quickly started going numb.

People filed in and out of a stopped train. I stared, knowing none of them would see what was happening to me. No one would notice evil right in front of their faces. Not until it was happening *to them*, would they care. A flash of blue caught my attention. A little bird flew inside one of the containers..

I blinked my eyes. The bird sat on one of the seats and started tapping on the window - tapping...at me? Was I hallucinating? I cranked my head, my leg disappearing more with each second. I swear that navy blue bird turned its head at me and nodded.

With every ounce of strength I could muster, I flung myself from the man's shoulders. I hit the ground, crushing my elbows and hip into concrete. I winced and climbed to my feet. I didn't know how he wasn't grabbing me. I pushed my feet into the pavement and screamed as I swung my arms in motion. I ran for that train. Or skipped, because I couldn't quite feel my leg enough to use it properly. The doors were closing. My one leg I could feel burned. My foot was numb. His steps were right behind me, the swish of leather deafening as he ran. I dared not look. The doors were barely open enough for me to fit through. I dove and his grimy freckled hand clenched onto my calf. And then... it was gone. The door shut on him, forcing him to pull back. I turned around, sitting as I stared out the window at his face. A face I don't think I'll ever forget.

He snarled his large upper lip and his eyes were nothing but pitch black pupils. Before he faded out of view, I saw the blood drip from his crooked nose. I must have elbowed him when I flung myself free.

And then...he was gone. I tried to get up, but my whole leg was now completely numb and I fell over. It took several minutes but I managed to hobble my way into the cart and climb into a maroon carpeted seat. People stared. But no one offered help. No one asked questions. I scowled back before remembering the bird. It wasn't at the window. I scanned the floors, seats, and tables, but the bird had vanished. The numbness climbed towards my face and my eyelids grew too heavy to keep open. Darkness shook my hand.

Then released me in Montana.

CHAPTER SIX

SOMETHING'S OUT THERE

Sometimes I wondered if that blue jay was an angel. Something about it made me brave for the first time in a long time. Brave enough to take a chance on life. Even if it was only a minute. But sometimes that's all we need to change the course of our lives. Sixty seconds to do the thing that terrifies us most.

The bed under me was soft, but not in a marshmallow comforting way, because my hips were not a fan. Wolf's fur tickled along the side of my cheek as I used his body for a pillow. My boots hung just over the edge, framing the view of pines and black walnut trees. Hues of orange, green, and red matched the warm painted sky as the sun inched beyond the horizon. Another vannie had entered the park an hour ago. A pair of hippies and their little avocado seed. If a seed had four chunky limbs and could gabber nonsense.

I didn't mind. So long as they kept to themselves and weren't the "let's be best friends because we both live out of our vehicles" sort of folk. I pulled my harmonica out from the shelf above my head. It glimmered, reflecting the last light of day. I turned it over in my hands. I didn't want to call attention to myself by playing it. As I closed my eyes, I placed it over my chest. I breathed in through my nose, bringing a lightness to my head. Other people were not going to dictate my actions.

I lifted the harmonica to my lips and played my favorite song. Which was the only one I knew. Faint voices sung the familiar lyrics to Tom Petty's 'You Don't Know How it Feels'. My scalp tingled and a shiver rippled down my shoulders, a sort of warm chill that made me happy. But happiness flew away all too quickly and heat flooded into the bridge of my nose. Trying not to cry, I turned my wandering mind back on the music I breathed.

I closed the doors as the last purple of twilight faded into black. A spark popped. I glanced down the way at my temporary neighbors. They sat around the glow of a pit fire, laughing. My imagination pictured the man with the dreadlocks catching the flame as he leaned over to kiss his girl. But in reality the fire never touched him. I smiled, hoping they were a fairy tale family. My smile dropped. Envy rose up like an unwelcome guest and I slammed my doors.

"Well Wolf, I better get to work, huh bud." Wolf looked up at me with his huge ice blue irises. The coloring on his eyebrows made it look as if he disapproved.

"What? The money for your food doesn't just pop into my bank account…" I narrowed my eyes and blinked. "Well…it does…but not without work."

He sighed. I scratched the top of his head and he wiggled until my fingers were under his left ear. I couldn't help the cackle I gave. His mouth hung open with a smile and I shook my head.

"Okay, I have to work now," I insisted and connected my mobile hotspot to my laptop while leaning over for my thermos. Water flew from my mouth when my chat blinked in bright bold white numbers that I had 15 new messages. I was at the end of a project that was due last night. *Great.* I grit my teeth and begrudgingly opened each one. Right as I finished reading the last panicked message from my client, the chatbox popped open.

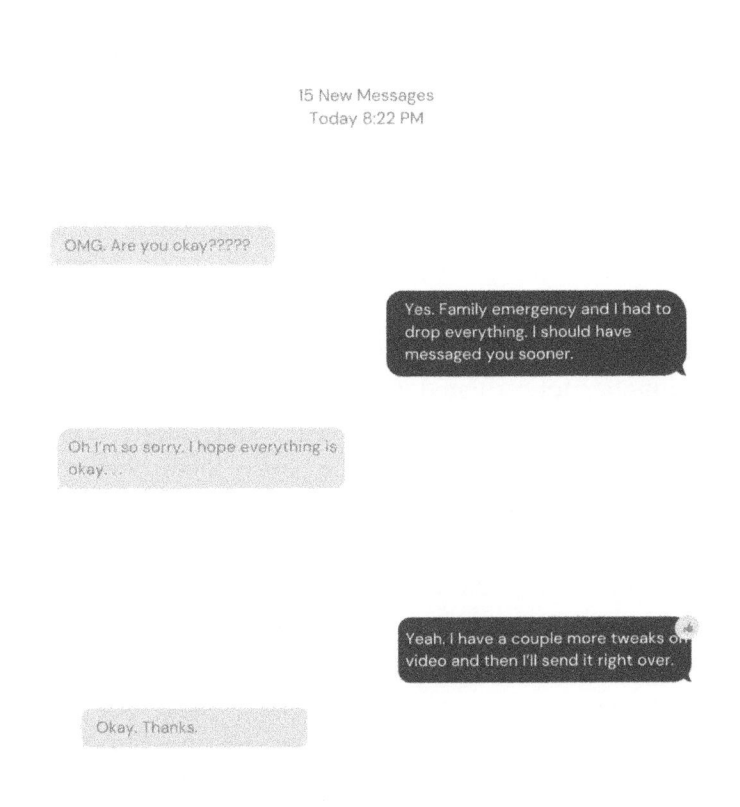

15 New Messages
Today 8:22 PM

OMG. Are you okay?????

Yes. Family emergency and I had to drop everything. I should have messaged you sooner.

Oh I'm so sorry. I hope everything is okay.

Yeah, I have a couple more tweaks on video and then I'll send it right over.

Okay. Thanks.

I slid the laptop from my lap to my mattress and stood up. It was going to be more than a few tweaks. I needed coffee. I wrapped my fingers on the mini counter, contemplating fixing some. If I wanted to get paid, I had to stay up to finish and submit my work to my client. But would the caffeine keep me awake after I was finished? What if that was what got me? And I was too tired to think clearly or fend for myself tomorrow. I flicked the water holder lid open. I wasn't being followed.

Four hours later, I glanced at the clock. *Not bad. Only 11:00 pm.* I rubbed my eyes and spent another ten minutes uploading the video files to my client. I really had to pee now. I rolled over and grabbed the revolver. I should've kept it on me more often but the damn thing dug into my skin. Maybe it was the holster. I only ever had enough to get what I needed, nothing more. My little van was a great representation of that. It wasn't as aesthetically pleasing as I'd like it to be. The walls were metal, not insulated wood. My only decorations were climbing ropes and carabiners that swung on metal hooks. The sink and counter were nothing more than an unwanted nightstand I found in a dumpster. I'd cut a hole through the center and plopped in a plastic tub. My van lacked all the pretty boho details that you see on Pinterest. But it was mine. My own little home and it was luxury in comparison to that first gnarly year in Montana when all I had were the clothes on my back.

Shaking the memories away, I grabbed my fur-lined denim jacket and threw it on over the hoodie I was already wearing. Each day grew colder and the night was worse. But the crickets still chirped. Their constant beeping grew louder when I opened the van's side door. Wolf raised his head. I flicked my head twice in the direction of the black wall of nature staring at us. Wolf whined as he stretched out of the bed and down to the asphalt. It almost sounded like he was talking…if words were comprised of "A wrooo wroo ooogh."

Coals still glowed from the pit fire. They were almost out but it was so dark that I could see them easily. It looked like the family was inside for the night. I walked around to the other side of my van. Not that anyone could see me, but it would be weird to not have some cover. I took a couple glances around me before dropping my pants and squatting. No way was I going to chance being too far from my van. And with it so dark out, lacking any sign of a moon, there was no need to find a bush.

As I zipped myself up, I froze at the sound of leaves crunching. I shook my head and buttoned my pants. It was probably Wolf. But when I turned around to walk to the other side of the van, Wolf trotted around the corner. His raised hair turned him into some kind of werewolf looking creature. He growled as I swiveled on my heels and yanked out my revolver. I stared into the forest, straining to see anything. I held my breath as I poised my gun out in front of me.

Crunch. I turned to the noise. It could be anything. Skunk, opossum, deer, bear, mountain lion. *Crunch crunch crunch.* My heart ping ponged against my rib cage. I still couldn't see anything. Wolf stood a few feet in front of me, growling into the darkness. I started backing up, gun still raised to the void. Silence. I gripped the revolver tighter. The wind howled and I swore I heard a whisper.

I turned and ran. My hands missed the door handle in my panic. I caught it and yanked it open.

"Wolf!" I screamed as I jumped in. He was there in seconds and I slammed it shut. My chest heaved up and down in an erratic rhythm that could only match the sound of dub step. Wolf's fur was still raised as he stared at the door. I tried to focus on slowing my heart while only breathing in through my nose.

I stood and grabbed my flashlight. With shaking hands, I pulled back the curtain and shined the light out the window. It gave a narrow tunnel of vision. Nothing. I climbed into the front seat and turned the headlights on. My heart was still going crazy in my chest. My mind started racing, bringing up all the old dusty memory files of every horror movie I'd ever seen.

I stared outside and clenched my silver revolver, until I heard Wolf slump to the floor. His fur had finally settled. I leaned back in my seat and flicked the headlights back off. Once my body calmed down, I realized my fingers and toes were numb from the cold. I climbed into my bed and kicked off my shoes before pulling another pair of socks over my feet and ducking under the covers. Wolf stayed on the floor, likely still worked up from what had just happened. Whatever had just happened.

I was going crazy. Every little thing had me on edge. I couldn't keep going like this. I needed to face whoever was coming for me. I glanced at the door. The pulse in my neck twitched. Goosebumps tingled up my arms. *But not tonight*, I thought. Needing a false sense of safety, I rolled away from the door and pulled the covers over my head.

CHAPTER SEVEN

PANIC

The thundering boom of an overly happy voice jerked me out of the trance I'd fallen under. Bright swirling lights glared on the maroon wall and I snapped my mouth shut. It had been half a lifetime since I'd set foot in a movie theater. I rubbed my eyes and tugged down my beanie before hunkering farther back in my seat, far left, top row. It was the best spot to survey everyone coming in.

The emptiness of the room was either proof of how insanely early I was, or how few people went to the theater in the middle of the week. Either way worked for my benefit.

The plan?

Figure out who was following me. Lure him to my van, where my revolver was resting on the floorboard of the front seat. Shoot him in the legs and put him in the back with Wolf. Then, as painfully as possible, extract the information. He wasn't my problem. No, it was whoever had hired him. I thought about killing the sick psycho hunting down a helpless young woman. But, they'd just send another. I was tired. Tired of hiding. Tired of running. Tired of being helpless.

Movement caught my eye at the bottom of the stairs. My chest heaved. A man in a ball cap looked my way. I turned my gaze back to the screen and gripped the armrest. I did my best to hold in all my unease, but it felt like I was about to shatter from the pressure with each step closer that he came to my row. Maybe I wasn't as tough as I thought. Maybe I should just end my worthless life. I shook the stupid voice away and bit as hard as I could down on my left cheek. Iron seeped down my throat.

"You okay?" he asked, taking a seat in the center of the top row. I looked him in the eyes. Why would he ask that?

"You look like you're in pain," he answered my unuttered question. I raised an eyebrow and turned away. I doubt he knew anything of pain. I also doubted he truly gave a damn. And sure enough I heard him empty his candy into his hand, moving on from continuing to pry. I glanced at my watch. Another twenty minutes left before the movie was set to start. From the corner of my eyes, he was doing nothing more than downing his Reeses Pieces while a trailer echoed in the far distance. Twenty more minutes. *Who the hell eats their candy that early?*

My heart began to skip to my stomach until it bubbled over like when you drop Mentos in soda. I stood. Perhaps too abruptly, and hurried down the steps, not pausing to see if he was following. I nearly ran into a mom and her two daughters as I rounded the corner. I muttered a sorry and picked up my pace. The door flung open like a fly swatter with my push. It took everything in me to not take off down the carpeted hall. Everything and a security guard walking my way.

He looked like he'd just stepped on a lego. I was that lego. He pushed his chin back, expecting what was about to come tumbling out of the freaked out girl's lips. I wanted to tell him. I wanted help. But what if he was the one after me? *Good disguise.* So I smiled, and kept walking, noting the security guards' shoulders fall. There was nothing he could do for me anyways.

Before I stepped out of the hallway and into the main area with the thick smell of buttered popcorn lingering in the air, I caught a door down the hall swing. I paused, waiting to see who was going to come out from behind the door. Only no one did. And I realized the security guard was no longer in the hallway.

"Wow," I muttered to myself. I was losing it. Absolutely gone. Paranoia was turning me into everything I didn't want to be. Weak, pathetic, vulnerable. *Victim.* I narrowed my eyes on the glass doors that led outside. Was he out there? Maybe waiting by my van? I couldn't let my fear cripple me. So I lifted my head, took a big breath and charged outside.

The onslaught from sunlight stopped me in my tracks. My pupils screamed. I squinted and raised my hand over my eyebrows. There was a short line in front of the ticket booth. Some of them glanced my way. I wondered what they thought but decided to ignore the intruding thoughts and gripped my nails into my palms.

My van sat at the end of the lot - big, dark blue, and obvious. The breeze whipped my hair into my face as I strode towards it. I thought for a moment I heard her name in that breeze, *Bridget*. My feet picked up their pace, controlled by the subconscious fear that I kept trying to shove away. I grit my teeth and ran.

It took three seconds to pull my keys from my pocket and hit the unlock button. Another ten to actually reach the door. I yanked it open and stretched for the cold metal on the floor board. Wolf's face popped around the driver's seat. I gripped my gun as I turned around for the first time since walking out of the hallway.

Nothing.

And I broke.

My legs gave way underneath me. My head rested against the open door, supporting me from completely collapsing on the asphalt. The tears poured like waterfalls. Before I could blink them away, Wolf was between my legs, pressing his chest to mine and licking my cheeks. He crushed his muzzle into my chest and wheezed. I dropped my gun back on the floorboard and wrapped my arms around his back, falling into the comfort of his soft fur. If only the moment could last a lifetime and I could feel this safe for forever.

CHAPTER EIGHT

LURE

I stared at the theater for nearly three hours, and yet the guy with the ball cap and fluffy hair still hadn't walked out those doors. I yanked off a piece of jerky and twisted my keys into the ignition. It roared to life with a refusal of a sputter. Then I clicked it off and shoved the keys back in my pocket. I had to go back in. I was going to end this. Wolf raised an eyebrow at me.

"What are you? A mind reader?" I asked him. He just slumped into the seat. *Here we go again.* If nothing happened, I only had one real option left. Return to the mountains. Get Brett's help. My stomach twisted at the thought. There was absolutely no way. Or I could just keep running, until I eventually got caught. The cold, hard fact remained - someone *was* looking for me. And they got close. But how close?

When I got to the booth to buy another ticket, the lady gave me a sideways look with her lips pursed together. I grabbed my ticket and hobbled as fast as I could down the hall, each step reminding me of my ankle.

I'd never heard of either of the movies I'd paid for today. Not like I was going to be watching them. As I rounded the corner to the hall, pinpricks crept up my legs. It wasn't that long ago that I was running from here. To say it was strange to be back was an understatement. A door to my right flew open and a wave of people flooded out. I pushed my arms deep into my sides and slid through the throng.

My movie was through the next door. Before I entered, I shot a glance behind me. No one. But I felt another chill as my hand touched the metal handle. Unease wrapped around me as I made my way up the ramp. It was only slightly darker in here but the whispers of people told me I wasn't as early this time.

My head felt light as I rounded the corner and looked up. *He* was there. At the top. What were the odds? I couldn't tell from this far, but he almost seemed to shift uncomfortably. Then, a small blue light lit up his face. He had a strong jaw even noticeable under his gruff, the kind that only men who worked out seemed to have. Which lessened my chance of running away.

Each foot grew heavier as I made my way up the steps. The light faded from his face and I wondered who he might have texted. I didn't look at him as I slid into the seat beside him. The whole left side of my body felt warm in such close proximity. The pounding in my head matched the one in my chest. I gripped the cup hole where a drink was supposed to go to keep myself from reeling away.

I still wasn't looking at him when he cleared his throat.

"You following me?" he asked. I scoffed.

"Cut the crap, we both know you're here for me."

He sat up, "What gave you that idea?"

"Please…" I shook my head. His eyes were a deep honey pot full of secrets. Was he really going to play this off like nothing?

"You see," he motioned with his hand, "I was here first. This time."

"Uh, huh." I rolled my eyes but inwardly felt the walls of confidence I had two seconds ago begin to crumble. He was right, how could he have known I'd come in here? It's not as if it was planned. Was he watching me? I flinched as he shifted in his seat.

"Whoah," he started, "I'm not gonna hurt you."

I scoffed, eliciting an eye roll from the baseball cap guy. I clenched my jaw as I stared at the fine bridge of his nose, wondering how easy it might shatter. Heat rose in my face and sulfur accumulated in my chest. My mind reeled at his words. Everyone hurts. It's what they do. It's human nature. There was no avoiding it. Eventually, even if he wasn't the one after me, he would hurt me. And that was a fact.

"Well, if you're not the one after me," I said as I stood, "then I have no use wasting time with you."

His mouth hung open, searching for the words. A comeback, an explanation, a rebuttal, a peace offering. Whatever it was, he was cut short as a small group of girls bustled up the steps, giddy and chattering loud enough to turn his attention.

I shook my head and side stepped down the aisle. I wanted to run, but my mind screamed at me to slow down. Perhaps he would follow. I paused at the bottom of the steps, took in a revolting breath of popcorn and dirty floors, and then glanced over my shoulders. He wasn't in the top row. I turned all the way behind me. But he wasn't on the stairs either. He had in a moment, entirely vanished. My hands started to shake like I'd downed five coffees.

I spun back around and turned the corner to the doors. What the hell was going on here? I pushed out the doors and into the hall. Empty. Was I losing my mind? Had insanity found me? Did my trauma finally push me over the edge? I strode down the hall, anger threatening to flood my face with salt droplets.

The hair on the back of my neck tickled. Footsteps pounded behind me. I didn't want to look. I needed to make my way to the van. This was it. This was my opportunity.

"Hey!" his voice called from my back. It *was* him. I only pushed harder into the floor, swiftly making my way out. But the fast pounding of his feet were close behind. He was running.

I picked up my feet and chucked for the main doors. I bowed my head in anticipation of the sunlight. I just had to get to the front seat. I just needed my gun. Nearly at my van, I looked up to see Wolf sitting in the driver's seat. He started barking and at first I thought he was excited to see me. But I realized his tone was vicious and only then did I hear the steps seconds behind me slapping against the asphalt, matching the quickening of my heart.

I turned around. My face smacked into cloth and my chest into the robust belly of a man, sending me backwards as I stumbled over my footing. I fell to the ground, my arm flinging out to the bumper.

My throat clenched inwards. I didn't recognize him.

"Stupid bitch," he said. I shuffled backwards, asphalt gripping into my palms as I attempted to get to my feet. His calves were larger than my head. If he sat on me, I'd die.

My breath heaved in and out, heavy and erratic. The stranger reached down and I attempted to skid out of the way. But his hand lay hold of my wrist, twisting it backwards. I screamed out from the pain and tried to kick him but my angle was off, my legs too short and I only swiped air. The momentum of my kick swung my body around and I somehow found myself on my stomach, in an even worse predicament.

I screamed again as something hard wrapped against the back of my head, pounding my face into the hot coal colored ground. The corners of my vision blackened. My head pounded, blocking out sound. I wanted to move but was too afraid of getting hit again.

Without warning, his hands flew from my back. Somewhere in the distance, I could hear shuffles and moans. I turned just as the stranger's face came crashing to the asphalt next to me, eyes closed, blood pouring from his nose into his mouth. Then, a different set of hands grabbed me. The grip was gentle while helping me to sit. My head swayed as I glowered at the puppy dog eyes in front of me.

CHAPTER NINE

PAYMENT

"You," I muttered, my brain still spinning. His palms held my face, steadying my bobble head.

"Are you okay?" He asked but all I could think about was that I kept smelling peanut butter and chocolate. His eyes were searching mine. I blinked and turned away, breaking his hold on my face. Even though his touch was gone, the warmth remained and I wanted to claw it away.

"I think so," I said. I tried to get to my feet but had to stop and let the darkness clear.

"I don't," he said and went to grab me.

"I'm fine!" I screamed far louder than I meant to as I swatted his hand away. He held them up and took a step back.

"I'm sorry," I said and pinched the bridge of my nose as he bent over and swept up his baseball cap. My cheeks were still warm from his touch.

"It's okay," he gave a weak smile.

I sighed, "What's your name?"

"Marshall," he held out his hand but I crossed my arms. I felt bad as his hand fell back to his side. "And you are?"

"Why did you come after me?" I asked, ignoring his question. He raised his eyebrows but then his attention was turned to the man on the ground who started grimacing.

"He was following you," he said. My heart lurched into my stomach. This was the guy after me. Without hesitation, I shoved my hand into his back pocket where a square outline was clearly visible.

"What are you doing?" Marshall asked. I paused before continuing to pull the wallet from his pocket.

"Finding out who he is, obviously," I stated.

"Obviously," he nodded and pulled out his phone.

"What are you doing?" I asked as I flipped open the wallet.

"Calling the cops," he stated. I stared at the name and picture on his drivers license then flipped to the dollar holder.

"Why?" I asked. I didn't feel like talking to cops. They couldn't help me.

"He just attacked you, why not?"

"I want answers."

"You can't just take that." he blurted when I stuffed the wallet into my own pocket. I rolled my eyes and leaned over the man's face. He was starting to come to. I gripped the back of his hair.

"Who are you working for?" I seethed. He responded with a grunt.

"I think we should let the cops handle this," Marshall said. I twisted to look up at him.

"You don't understand. The cops aren't going to help."

"Yes, they are," he returned. I stood up. I couldn't hide the glare on my face.

"How would you know?" I asked. Marshall was about to say something when the man suddenly stood and bolted off, dodging between cars. Marshall took off after him but lost him across the busy street as horns blasted their annoyance. I stared, amazed he didn't get hit. And then I screamed out a curse. I was back at the start. He'd come after me again.

At least I had a name now. And knew what he looked like.

I swung open the van door and Wolf nearly tackled me. He jumped up and slobbered his tongue over my entire face. Blinded, I grabbed for his leash.

"Still calling the cops?," I yelled to Marshall as he sauntered back my way. He looked about as agitated as I felt.

"No," he said. I didn't respond. I wasn't sure how to. There was no point in calling the cops now but something about his sudden drop of tone twisted my stomach into knots.

"There's a cafe over there," Marshall started as I eyed him from the corner of my vision while Wolf sniffed out a pee spot.

"If you want some tea or something…calming…"

"I told you I was fine," I reminded him.

"How are you handling that so well?"

I pounded my fist against the side door, "I'm not. I'm totally freaking out and trying not to focus on the fact that I'm freaking out."

"Uh, huh. So chamomile then?"

I turned back towards his grinning face, "Fine. You got me. But just a drink, that's it."

He held up his hands, "Just a drink."

I sighed, did I really just agree to a drink? What was wrong with me? I could still back out. Change my mind. There was nothing wrong with that. Yet as this knight in shining armor of a man looked at me, my walls began to crumble. The putter in my heart was an entirely new feeling. It should have comforted me. I should be happy. But I didn't like it. I didn't like someone so easily sneaking their way into my heart. So he saved me. A man could do a good deed. Me agreeing to a drink was nothing more than a way to repay him for his kindness.

That was all.

"I'm Jay," I said and for a second the color seemed to drain from his face, but then he smiled.

"Nice to meet you, Jay."

I mumbled back with a half smile. Wolf returned to my side, waiting for the command to attack. But I didn't need to give it. Not yet.

"Where to?" I asked

"There's a place across the way, I saw it trying to get that guy." He tipped back on his heels and shoved his hands into his jacket pocket. I contemplated my decision as I stared across the traffic.

"Okay, but I don't imagine they welcome dogs," I said

Marshall smiled, "No probably not."

My palms felt sticky against the door handle. I snapped my fingers for Wolf to jump inside. He hesitated, big dopey eyes questioning my sanity. I snapped my fingers again and he hopped in.

"Kay, bud. I'll be right back." I rubbed his head and leaned forward, our foreheads meeting against each other in a moment's pause. He was unbelievably comforting. You'd think he was trained for this. But he was a sickly runt, dropped into the hands of a girl who didn't even have a home, and we were just two broken souls coming together.

When I shut the van door, I came face to face with my reflection. My oat colored hair flew in frazzled clumps around my neck. I quickly smacked at it, attempting to smooth it down, wishing I could do something about my thick, almost unibrow, crawling across the bridge of my nose. Although it was far less noticeable than the giant lump on my forehead and the gash over my cheek. I grit my teeth as the pain entered my mind for the first time.

"Okay, all set," I said, turning around. Marshall looked up with a grin on his face. Maybe it was the crease on his forehead, but something told me he was uneasy. Nerves? He couldn't possibly be nervous. With ease, he glided my way. I felt my throat tighten. And then he walked past, almost brushing my shoulder. I exhaled and imitated his pace as we made our way to the sidewalk.

"Why's it your favorite?" his voice cut through the silence and I nearly jumped.

"What?"

"Anything…" he said.

"I must have hit my head harder than I realized because I have no idea what you're talking about." I rocked forward on my toes as we waited for the light to turn green.

"Right. Then, something easy, favorite ice cream flavor."

I laughed, "You think about ice cream while it's this cold out?" I puffed out a cloud of my breath. It hovered in the air like smoke.

"I think that's what made me think about ice cream."

"Right. Let's see. Ice cream….Ice cream….Death by Chocolate." It'd been a long time since I had ice cream.

"That is a good flavor," he smirked.

"And yours?" I returned the question.

"Vanilla."

"Vanilla?"

"You can't beat a classic." Marshall put his shoulders back, towering even higher. I craned my neck looking up. He had to be 6'2. No, 6'4? Anything seemed giant to my little 5'1" frame.

"Seems a little boring." I shrugged. It sounded flat, but in all honesty, I didn't mind boring. Predictability was comforting.

"And you live life on the edge?" he asked, jumping up the curb as if it were an enormous block.

"What makes you think that?"

"Living out of a van. Or the gun under your shirt," he said.

"You can tell?!" I scoffed and stretched my shirt further over my waist.

"What exactly was it you were doing today?" He raised an eyebrow. I felt stuck. The words melted in my mouth and turned to gum between my teeth.

"Nothing," I lied. "I was just minding my own business when I got attacked."

"Except you knew you were being followed beforehand? Makes sense."

"Women can never be too careful can they?" I pointed the question back at him. His hand slid into a golden handle of a building we were passing. He yanked back and stood with the door open. A warm draft mixed with coffee and caramel hit my face.

"After you." Ah, he was charming. I should have known.

CHAPTER TEN

INVITATION

The low hum of chatter permeated through ceramic clinks. Bell shaped lights glowed orange against a red wall. I made my way through the tables and found a seat. Marshall came up behind me and pulled out the chair before I had a chance to say anything. I gave a slight smile before sitting. He was overdoing it. But the flutters in my stomach were protesting the nagging in my head.

"So," he said as I traced my finger along the smooth inner side of a mug handle.

"So…" I echoed back. The chamomile scented steam drifted around my nose as I raised the drink to my lips. It was calming. Marshall chose coffee…only to dump the entire cafe's supply of creamer in it. I grimaced watching him enjoy it.

"I'm sorry if I scared you earlier. I didn't mean to."

I waved him away, "You didn't do anything." I was overreacting and paranoid.

He raised an eyebrow and changed the subject, "You said someone was after you."

"Yeah, and he got away," I cleared my throat, maybe not so paranoid.

"Mmm," he muttered, "he did."

I swiveled my head to the large wall length window behind us. He was out there, somewhere, waiting for me. When would he attack again? I couldn't be sure. I rubbed the rim of my sleeve between my fingers. Was Wolf okay? He wouldn't go after my dog, would he?

"You're going to be okay," Marshall said, noting my sudden unease.

I took a sip, "Yeah, how would you know?"

But before he could answer, a waitress brought us a small plate of iced cinnamon rolls. I refused to take one. Even if they looked delectable. I only promised a drink. Marshall snagged one up before the waitress had even turned back around.

He held a finger to his lips as he chewed, "I'm not going to let anything bad happen to you on my watch."

"Why? You don't even know me," I said and tugged at my beanie.

"You're right," he leaned back, "So tell me. Who are you Jay?"

I took another sip, hoping it might calm my nerves, "What would you like to know? I'm not that interesting."

"I doubt that." He paused, "Okay, something easy…favorite movie?"

"Dirty Harry."

His eyes shot wide, "Really?"

"Of course," I said and finally reached for one of the cinnamon rolls, caving to the roar of my stomach.

"Okay, why Dirty Harry?"

"He's just a stand up guy that does right and takes no BS. I wish I could be more like him," I said.

He nodded, thinking about it, "I like that. So how are you not like Harry?"

I grit my teeth, "I'm afraid of people, afraid of being seen a certain way, afraid of standing up for myself." I almost whispered that last part, reflecting on my life and how many times I didn't fight against being used. How many times I so easily followed suit, did what I was told, even when it was killing me. Even when it was wrong.

"I would have never guessed that about you," he said.

I crossed my arms, "And why's that?"

"You seem set in who you are and what you think. I certainly didn't get any impression you were a people pleaser."

I tipped my head, "Maybe not so much anymore, I had to learn the hard way." Marshall's eyes fell to the floor as if I had struck some kind of nerve. His whole body seemed devoid of air.

"What about you?" I asked, curious now more than ever.

He came to life as if nothing had happened, "Predator."

I raised an eyebrow, "So you're a fan of classics too."

"Oh you know, guns, aliens, macho men," he flexed for emphasis, "and extremely quotable lines."

I laughed, "Extremely quotable. Whatever happened to movies?"

"Not much to work with these days," he chuckled back.

"Not that I would know, I don't watch much anymore," I said

"And your trip to the movie theater was to remedy that?"

I bit my lip, realizing my slip, "Yes, exactly. That's exactly what I was doing - what movie was it I ran out on by the way?"

He laughed and I joined in for the first time in a while. The tension drained from my body. For the first time in a very long time, maybe ever, I was enjoying myself in somebody else's company. I couldn't, however, ignore the erratic bouncing of his knee that never ceased. I thought about asking him about it, but it could just be an anxious tic. I had my fair share of them myself, as I tugged at my sleeves and beanie about every two minutes.

"You okay?" he asked, catching me peering out the window behind me. Again. His eyes narrowed as I flipped around to face him.

"Yeah," I cleared my throat. He was still out there. I flicked a crumb from my black jeans.

"No, actually, no I'm really not," I admitted.

"Do you want to talk about it?" Marshall leaned forward.

"I was just thinking about Wolf. I should get back." I told him, hopefully deflecting any more questions. I was getting too comfortable.

"Yeah," he nodded, "We have been here a while."

"Poor guy has been in there all day. I'm gonna have to run him." I laughed, thinking of his pent up energy.

"Run him? You're gonna run?" Marshall asked as we both stood.

"Maybe," I shrugged. It would've been better to have found a trail to hike. But the last time I did that a bear attacked me.

"Want some company?" he asked. I bit the inside of my lip. Did I? What was I going to do if the guy showed up again? Suddenly the idea of having more back up sounded very appealing. Marshall already came to my rescue once, like some kind of knight in shining armor. I tilted my head at him. What are you? I wanted to ask, but instead I smiled and said, "Sure."

"So is that a yes?" he questioned as we walked towards the trash can, "Because if it's not a definite yes, I don't want to impose."

I swallowed.

"You look two shades paler," he noted and tossed our trash

in the bin.

"I doubt that is possible." I laughed with a half smile. And he opened the door, but I didn't answer his question. Maybe I wanted to see what he would do. Or maybe I just sucked at words. And speaking. And acting like a normal socialized human being.

"Soooo?"

I swallowed and slid past his torso, out of the building, into the cold. The warmth of his body heat wavered through the air to brush me. Or maybe that was the blood rushing through my body. Pins pricked my feet as I walked. My chest rose as I straightened my back out of the familiar hunch it liked to curve to.

"Yes," I said finally. He raved. There was a skip to his step that was missing moments ago. A new found enthusiasm. I wondered why. Why the looming sadness and anxiety seemed to have vanished. Maybe it was all in my head before. Maybe the sadness and anxiety was my own.

I shot a look behind me, the feeling of being followed still tearing at the edges of my sanity. The concrete street was flourishing with people, all too concerned to care to look at one another. Each one clutching their sweater or coat or scarves. Everyone was affected by the sudden drop in temperature. I tucked my hands into my jean pockets. I was was affected by something else entirely.

"Okay," Marshall said, "Another favorite...How do you feel about the seasons?"

"Winter's my favorite," I said without pause.

"So," Marshall started and pressed the crosswalk button, "Why exactly is winter your favorite season?"

I grit my teeth and the light blinked green. A million things floated through the vastness of my mind. Too much to utter. Too much to confess.

Should I reveal the truth? What would his reaction be if he knew? He waited patiently for my answer, as if he'd spent the last hour doing so. Okay with my slowness. Okay with me.

"I like to wear layers and all other seasons are too hot for that," I said. Part truth. My gut was telling me not to reveal too much. And by gut, I mean past experiences. Truth was, that beneath all those layers, was the scar I fought to hide.

CHAPTER ELEVEN

DOG FIGHT

A dandelion danced in the wind until a car tire squished it into the mud. The abrupt shutting of a metal door brought my eyes to Marshall's. He was smiling, softly, as if something was on the fringe of ruining his day. I let out a sigh. His car wasn't green. I didn't want to think about what I'd do if it were. My throat began to tighten as I contemplated the idea. But I quickly brushed it aside. Of course Marshall wasn't after me. The other guy that pounded me into the asphalt was. But I was skeptical of Marshall. Reality screamed that there were no such things as good men. For a moment, I wanted to frolic in the fairy tale and ignore the pain in my gut telling me something wasn't right.

"Hi," I winced into the setting sun.

"How are you feeling?" he asked. *Why did he make me want to scream and hold my breath all at once?*

"I feel a migraine setting in," I admitted and opened the door for Wolf. He instantly hopped out and sat by my feet, waiting for the click of the leash. Once on, he forced his way in front of me. Between Marshall and I. I bent over and scratched behind Wolf's ear and he leaned into my hand.

"He's stunning," Marshall commented, tucking his fists into his pockets. I looked up and smiled.

"Yeah. You can pet him if you'd like," I said.

"That's okay," he said.

I squinted, "Not a dog person?" There. Something negative.

"No, dogs are great." He shook his head as he opened the gate to the park.

"Then….."

"He needs to be certain I'm safe for you before trusting me to touch him." Damn. My jaw must have dropped open because Marshall chuckled. I felt my throat tighten again, but this time it wasn't out of fear. I looked towards the clouds, trying to keep the tears in my eyes from falling out. I breathed in the crisp air and looked back at Marshall. All I could do was smile as I plopped down on one of the benches.

Wolf circled me three times before sitting at my feet, unamused by the dalmatian and two pit bulls in the park with him.

"Go on, bud, I'll be fine!" I told him, waving my arms in encouragement. He leaned his head back around me, eyebrows down in disbelief.

"Go," I insisted. He huffed. A few seconds later he was up and meandering around the benches.

"This is why I have to run," I muttered. Marshall elicited a deep chuckle before pulling his ball cap more snug over his tousled hair. I wrapped my arms around me as I noted the veins in his hands. *Were they were as prominent in his forearms?* I shook the thought away. I didn't need to be thinking like that.

"You have a ball or something?" he asked, knocking me out of my semi trance.

"A frisbee, but good luck getting him to go after it," I snorted.
"Doesn't want to leave your side, huh?"
"Never."
"I feel like there's a story there," Marshall egged. I picked the ends of my hair up, examining the split ends in the orange glow beaming through the tall brick apartments around us.
"It's boring," I said, warning him. He waved me off as if that statement were ridiculous.
"Why don't we walk and you tell me."
"Why?" I asked as he stood.
"Because you said Wolf needs to run off pent up energy and he won't leave your side."
"No, I mean…why are you doing this? Why do you care? Don't you have something to do today?" The questions fell out one after the other. He sighed and looked to his left before answering.
"I only work Monday through Thursday," he shrugged, "and I just want to make sure you're okay."
I snorted, "Why?"
"Is it so hard to believe that someone can care for another person simply because?"
"Yes, yes that is hard to believe" I stated. Harder than he could know.
He paused for a long moment, "I guess you're right."
"Oh?" Was all I could choke out, I was expecting him to fight back, not confirm my position. He stood and held out his hand. I stared at it momentarily before standing without his help. Disappointment flashed across his face as he dropped his arm.
"Sorry," I whispered
"Don't be," he waved me off.
"No, I don't want to be mean…" I started, feeling my pulse

quicken, "I- I just don't like to be touched. I'm sorry."

"Like I said, don't be. It's okay." He smiled and my chest deflated.

"Thanks. For everything," I said as we started walking. He grinned and nodded his head. For a second, I swore It looked like he clenched his jaw.

"He was a runt." I blurted after we walked the fenceline in silence.

"Huh?"

"Wolf, he was a runt in a litter. The couple I got him from gave him as payment to me for a job I did. But I didn't know anything about dogs and I was kinda homeless at the time so he was severely underweight with worms and pretty sick that first year."

"That doesn't sound like good payment," he winced. My stomach turned remembering how much we both struggled.

"The couple had no idea I was homeless...Or maybe they did and thought I needed a companion. As hard as it was, I can't imagine that time without him," I shrugged before continuing, "and I guess that instilled loyalty in him."

"Struggling together does that," he kicked up some dirt as we made our way around the park, hanging close to the fence.

"I suppose so," I sighed.

We continued walking for close to an hour before taking a break back at the benches. Marshall rocked and I glanced away when his eyes met mine. I couldn't allow myself to fall for someone, even if they were kind and rudely attractive. In a moment we'd say our goodbyes and I'd never see him again. That's what I wanted, I tried to convince myself. Wolf's love and devotion would always be enough...because I couldn't allow anyone too close again. I rubbed my arms as the sunlight moved away, leaving us in the shade of the evening. It felt too cold, even for the shade. Dark clouds were rolling in from the west, swirling in shades of gray.

"Look," Marshall's voice made me jump.

"I haven't been completely honest," he said with a pause between each word. My eyes darted to his knee. Bouncing again.

"Okay..." I said, mimicking his pace. I pulled my lips in and clenched my fists, anticipating the punch.

"There's something I need to tell you. And it isn't going to be easy, but please, don't freak out." The words came out fast, rolling off his tongue in hiccups and heat rushed to my face. My breath caught in my chest. What was he about to confess?

"I'm with-" but before he could finish his sentence, a loud shriek pierced our ears. I turned my head so fast, something in my neck popped. I winced and slapped my palm to my neck. The pain quickly dissipated as shrieks and barks continued to echo.

Marshall was standing. The large crowd of people were yelling as two of the dogs tore into each other, blood obvious on the dalmatian's fur. One of the girls, who looked like a teenager, was crying as she tried to jump in and pull her dog away. But an older, dark-skinned, gentleman yanked her back. Wolf stood in front of me, barking at the chaos before us. I laced my fingers through his collar, not wanting him to get in the middle.

"Take him back to your van," Marshall instructed, "I'll stay here and make sure everything is okay." I nodded and tugged at Wolf who fell into my leg, circled me around and then trotted with me back to the gate. I closed it quickly behind me and clicked Wolf's leash on.

My breath was raspy and winded. A giant gust whipped through my hair and jacket, causing me to shiver. Nothing could be made out yet through the tangle of a crowd of people and dogs. The shrieking barks had subsided, but I could still hear the girl crying and I felt a lump in my throat.

I couldn't imagine her pain right now, seeing something she loved hurt. I'd never experienced that, I thought as I climbed into my van. I was always the one being hurt. Wolf circled my legs before jumping up on the mattress.

As I waited for Marshall to return, snow flurries fell like ash outside the window. My fingers were ice picks as I tried to blow my breath over them. I shoved them into my pockets and was met by the unfamiliar wallet. Without procrastination, I jerked it out and stared at the picture. His name was Ricky Salvador and he was born in 1983. The only other thing in the whole wallet were a few twenty dollar bills. I pulled everything out and slipped it into my own square money holder. Still freezing, I set them on the counter and plugged in my kettle, hoping it would heat up the water faster than normal. That's when I heard Wolf shift on my bed.

"What?" I asked at his intense stare with his ears standing on pointed alert. I plopped myself down beside him and he moved his jaw over the top of my lap. His warmth was comforting. As the water in the kettle began to roll, so did the reel of events from today in my mind. I'd failed. And if it hadn't been for Marshall…

I didn't want to think about it. But my mind didn't care about my heart, and the thoughts of what could have been, forced a burning sensation in my eyes. I felt so utterly pathetic and helpless. It was only a matter of time. Soon enough, they'd find me. And I was afraid there would be nothing I could do about it.

CHAPTER TWELVE

GUNFIRE

The day went by so fast it was as if the sudden blizzard had pushed more than just the wind. It had pushed time, too.

I kept glancing out the window where streetlights glowed through the falling snow in the dim evening. The streets wore a thin layer of white over them and if I tilted my head, I could see that the tops of the awnings did too.

My kettle clicked off, alerting me that the water was hot. I slipped two hot cocoa packets out of my little covered shelf. The smell was uplifting. Sweet chocolate in hot water. Not as good as milk, but a million times better than bland tea. I held my hands over the two mugs, letting the steam warm them up.

"This is stupid, why don't I just turn the car heater on?" I muttered to myself. My mind was too frazzled from the day to think rationally apparently. Touching the lump on my forehead, I wondered if that was more literal than I'd like. I pushed the thought aside and made for my way over the center console.

A sudden rap at the door made me jump and drop the keys. They fell perfectly down the side of the driver's seat. *Damn.*

I opened the door to see Marshall with snowflakes on his

shoulders.

"Oh my god, aren't you cold?" I asked as I realized he only had a light sweater on. He shook his head. I looked around behind him, but I couldn't see anyone. I didn't know what happened to the other people. The dogs. The chaos.

And Marshall was just standing there looking like he saw a ghost.

"What?" I asked, not alluding to what I was asking. I blinked hard and started over.

"What happened, is everything alright? What's wrong?" Bells started ringing in my head and I backed up. Marshall cleared his throat.

"It's…fine. Everyone is fine. It wasn't as bad as it looked. Are you okay?" his voice was shaken, not confident and smooth like before. I tried to ignore it.

"Yeah…yeah, I'm good. I made some cocoa. Here." I grabbed the mugs of chocolatey goodness and the steam wafted up to my face. I smiled. But Marshall's lips were a hard line. Wolf had slid off the bed in the most dramatic way. I wanted to laugh but Marshall's face worried me.

"Look, why don't you come inside, warm up, have some liquid happiness, and tell me what's up." I nodded towards where I was crouching over, because even with my height disadvantage, there was still not enough headspace.

"I- I don't think that's a good idea."

"Oh, come on, I know you're super chivalrous and like prince charming but you're freezing, it's okay."

"It's not that."

"I don't care what it is," I said, feeling frustration raise my voice an octave, "You're gonna be an ice sculpture soon." He didn't say anything. When his jaw pulsed from clenching it, my grip on the handles tightened.

"Fine, here, at least take this, warm up your hands."

He lifted his palms up, "No, I've done enough."

"What are you talking about?" He wouldn't answer, just shook his head, like he couldn't form the words.

"Marshall?"

"Look Bridget," He blurted in near rage, "I'm sorry, I can't. I can't get in there with you. I can't take anything from you. I shouldn't even be here right now in this damn weather. This should have ended hours ago. We need to talk."

"What did you just say?" I didn't even hear the rest of his words. The words past Bridget. My hands went numb and the mugs clashed at my feet. Searing hot chocolate splashed up to my knees but I didn't feel it. All I could feel was the pounding in my chest, the tightening of my throat, the panic in my cells. My vision started to cloud around the edges. I barely saw Marshall - or the look of shock in his eyes as he backed up. As he realized what he said.

"Jay, wait, it's not what you think," he said, his hands reaching for me but I shook my head and backed into the wall. I wanted to scream but I could only take a sharp inhale that stuck in my chest.

I can't breathe, I can't breathe, I can't breathe! I clutched at my sternum as tears poured out of my face, unable to stop what was about to happen. He was going to grab me. He was going to stuff me in his car. I was going back to Seattle. I was going back to hell.

I couldn't. I wouldn't. I pulled the gun from my hip. Marshall's face changed and I couldn't pull the trigger fast enough. His hands moved quicker than I could blink and suddenly he was holding the revolver. *Dear God, help me.*

In my panic I didn't hear Wolf. I didn't see him move in front of me. But when his deep growl screeched into a menacing ear piercing bark, I noticed. I noticed Marshall back up again. His eyes were glossed over and his left palm was raised as he held the gun in his right.

"I don't want to hurt her," but Wolf wasn't listening. His teeth were slashing towards the threat. I still couldn't breathe and I could barely see. What I *could* see was shaking, like the world was falling apart. I was falling apart. I was the one shaking.

And Wolf leaped. Into the frost. Into the storm. Straight for Marshall's throat.

"NO!" I screamed and flung my body outside, but the bullet was faster than me. I felt it long before I heard it. My body slammed against the ground and my head whipped against the back tire. Pain radiated from my hip, down my leg. I tried to catch my breath as Wolf whimpered beside me and my ears ruptured with an explosion from the bang.

"Fuck!" Marshall yelled above me.

"Oh God, no," he whispered, crouching so close I could feel his body heat. I knew he was touching me, near my hip, where the bullet punctured, but the hot sharp pain exploding through me kept me from caring.

"Don't move," Marshall spat, as if I could, "I'm going to get help." He reached into his pocket for his cell. But after two minutes, and a few cuss words, he slammed it against his thigh and swiveled his head around. Finally, air eased its way back into my lungs, but my vision was colored mustard.

"Wolf," I whispered. I could barely touch him with the tips of my fingers.

"Look, I have no service. I have to go for help." He went to leave, terror still in his eyes.

"I'll be right back, I promise," he said. But I didn't give a damn about his promises. He ran off, his steps crunching in the snow. I craned my neck as far as I could to see Wolf. His fur wasn't white. It was crimson. And that was the last I saw before everything went black.

CHAPTER THIRTEEN

STRANGE SURROUNDINGS

The world was obsidian. A faint song danced in the air. A lull to match the aching sorrow that had become me. I strained to listen closer, but the melody faded and a mechanical hum swirled in its place. My eyelids felt like they were weighed down. The room was dim, lit only by a faint glow in the corner.

I blinked several times, trying to clear the fuzz. The glow was coming from a small white lamp on a dresser across the room. My peripheral vision was distorted and it felt like I was looking through pretend binoculars. I knew I was in a bed. In a small room. In someone's home. Next to the dresser was a single wood bookshelf stuffed full with thick spines and gold lettering. The quilt over me smelled of lavender and allspice. Beneath a little cream tea towel, black and white pictures of strangers lined the top of the bedside table beside me.

When I tried to move, it felt like someone stuck a hot iron through my side. I grimaced, trying to hold in my shout. My lungs seized as every muscle in me clenched at the intrusion. I bit down on my bottom lip. Slowly, each part of me released as the pain melted and my breath came back in stutters.

A new song lingered in the doorway and the world clouded

into darkness again as voices swirled around me. Unfamiliar and strange. I tried to jerk away when cold hands fluttered at my side. I wanted to run. I needed to escape - but my body refused to cooperate and the room melted away along with the rushed jumbling of words I couldn't understand.

A line of light gradually moved across my face until it rested over my eyes. It was warm and familiar. Sunlight. I blinked. All familiarity vanished. I had no idea where I was. The smell of lavender and allspice jerked the memory of this plain room, and the pain, into my mind's forefront.

Wolf.

Where was he? I threw off the quilt, not giving time to question where I was or acknowledge the stabbing in my side. I froze. My black jeans were gone. In their place was a skirt that reached my ankles. It felt like being stuck in a cocoon. The shirt on me was different too. Maroon. It came up to my collarbone and the sleeves were only three quarters. They didn't reach my wrists. They didn't cover the mark. My chest began to twitch with panic. I could feel heat rush to my face.

I closed my eyes. *Deep Inhale. I can do this.* I swung my legs over the side of the bed with gritted teeth. *Exhale.* I clutched onto the bedpost and shoved myself up. I didn't care where I was, but I wasn't staying. I was going to find Wolf. I was getting out. Nothing was going to stop me. Not even a bullet wound.

I slid towards the door and attempted to turn the handle without making a sound. But it was old and old things are noisy. It creaked, and creaked again when I swung the door open. I faced a hallway. To the right was nothing but a wall and another door. To the left was an open corner, but I couldn't see what was around it. Was Marshall going to be there? Waiting for me? Or worse? Marshall had delivered me to the trafficker.

I took a deep breath and crept out. The floor was cold beneath my socks. My head felt light and my stomach was acting as if I was at an amusement park. I swallowed back my fear. I just had to make it to the front door. Figure out where I was. Get back to the park. I made it to the corner and crept my head out, just enough to see. It opened out into a kitchen with an island and bar on the left and an empty living room on the right. I breathed. At the very end, right in front of me, was the door. I started.

A creak sounded behind me, around the corner. *Shit, shit, shit.* I pushed with everything I had to get to that door but I was being pulled back, stopped. I swiveled my head around. The skirt had caught a wicker basket of blankets. I yanked the skirt loose, toppling over the basket with a thud. I inhaled fast. Footsteps were echoing behind me but I didn't look. I grasped the door handle and yanked it open.

A blast of icy wind smacked me in the face. I pushed against it. The steps were covered in snow and I had no shoes on. In my hurry to get out I didn't think to look for my shoes. All

I cared about was getting out. And here I was, out, but not free. Someone was behind me. I could feel them. I moved into the freezing white mounds. Pain shot down my leg as I went down a step. I couldn't help the shout that escaped my mouth. My hand shot out to the railing and ice water seeped into the laceration at my ankle.

"Woah, sport," a woman's voice laughed beside me. The sweet crisp smell of peaches flitted through the air when she wrapped her hands around my shoulders. I shook free and hobbled down another step. Undeterred, she jumped in front of me, far more ambulatory than I was capable of in my condition. Far more graceful too, even though she was wearing the same thing I was - a dreadful long pencil skirt. Though her stomach protruded just enough to signal curious minds. She held her palms up in front of me... the same way Marshall had.

"Move," I ordered through gritted teeth. And she did. Towards me.

"Hey, it's okay. I know. You don't know me," her words were soft, "you don't know where you are. You're scared. I get it. But it's better if you were resting right now." Her eyes glimmered in the morning sun, gold as honey, and again I thought of Marshall. I shook my head, I was not going to fall under her trance.

"No, I need to find my dog." I moved forwards and attempted to brush past, but she held my shoulders, firm yet somehow delicate. I expected her to shove me back inside. Back to that bed. Away from my escape.

But instead she loosened her grip and asked, "Your dog?"

"Yes," I said, tears hanging on the edge of my eyes. I was trying to hold them in. I didn't know this woman and I didn't want her to see any weakness. But my mind was tormenting me and it was hard to resist. I had to get to Wolf. I had to help him. He was shot, too.

Her voice washed over me and pulled me away from the dark thoughts, "Was he with you when you were shot?"

I nodded.

Her light brown eyebrows furrowed with thought for a moment.

"I don't remember any dog," she said, "but I understand." She glanced over her shoulder and I followed her gaze, realizing now exactly where I was. Just beyond the street, down a ways, sat the park. It wasn't far, but we were on the backside and from here, I couldn't see the parking lot. It was hidden behind a mini forest of trees.

"Yoav!" the woman shouted, causing a jump from me.

"Is she coming inside?" a man's voice sounded behind me. The accent was different. I wasn't sure, but maybe middle eastern?

"No, no, no. Can you bring me Bubbe's wheelchair?" She asked him. He didn't answer, but I could hear footsteps retreating inside and moments later returning.

"Ah, todah!" She smiled big and warm and her barely visible crow's feet deepened.

"If you are not going inside," the man said as he opened up the chair, "Where do you intend to be going...of all days?"

"We are looking for her dog," she smiled with a nod at me. I didn't return the smile.

"A dog? But why?" he sounded confused, as if dogs were as much of a pest as mice.

"Because a worried heart does not let the body heal...or *rest*," she stated, "besides, we're not going far. Just to where we found her."

"Okay," he sighed. Realizing that somewhere in the midst of that conversation, the woman had let go of me, I finally turned to see who she was talking to. Middle Eastern was correct. His long curly side things swung back and forth as he climbed the slick steps back into the house and shut the door. I'd never seen an orthodox jew in pajamas. I don't know why I assumed they wore those black suits all the time. Of course they didn't.

"Now," the woman said to me, "If you sit, I will take you where you want to go."

CHAPTER FOURTEEN

GONE

The incandescent sun did nothing to prevent me from shivering. I felt like a prisoner in that wheelchair, pathetic and out of control. But I was going in the direction I wanted…for now. I held my breath as we rolled closer. Would Wolf be there? Would his body be cold and lifeless? My heart seized and my vision fogged. *Stop Stop Stop.* I bit my lip and blinked away the misty haze.

When we turned around the bend, past the large grouping of trees covered in a layer of melting snow, an empty lot came into view, and my throat fell into my stomach.

"Where is it?!" I wanted to scream as I gripped the handles of the wheelchair so hard that my knuckles went white. The lot was completely empty. Wolf wasn't there. And neither was my van.

"This is where we found you," the woman whispered.

Tears rolled down my cheeks. I tried to blink away my reality. Yet, the only thing where my van should have been was blood stained asphalt. I started to hyperventilate, ragged breaths wheezing in and out like an accordion.

"Maybe he's walking around, we can walk and see if we can find him," she offered.

"My van is gone too…" I breathed.

"It must have been towed away," the woman pointed to a sign that read, "No parking after 10pm." But that didn't explain where Wolf was. Maybe he was okay. I tried to spot his gray and white fur in the park. But row after row of empty red apartment buildings and my hope withered.

It was useless. I couldn't see Wolf, just like before the bear attacked. A chill crawled down my spine. My forearms prickled in gooseflesh. Everything was wrong. There were no bears here, but I knew there was something just as deadly.

I couldn't hold it in any longer, my body shook uncontrollably as sobs found their way out of my chopped vocal chords. I wish I'd died in that parking lot. Why did they save me? Why didn't they save Wolf? Another shriek left my body. I covered my face in my hands.

Where was Marshall?

He caused all of this.

"It's gonna be okay, we'll figure this out," the woman gripped my hand in between hers.

I yanked it back, "Don't touch me!"

She stepped away as I stared into her eyes. There was no fear, no shock or surprise. Sadness lingered there for so long I had to look away. Why did I feel bad? I didn't know her. She could be evil. She could be *one of them*.

I grit my teeth. Tear lines continued to stain my cheeks. I didn't care enough to wipe them away. I just wanted my life back. A life I was trying to find. One that was robbed from me as a child. And was being threatened now. No, we were past threatening. All at once it came crashing down, destroyed. I was plunged into a lake under ice. And I was drowning.

In through the nose, out through the mouth. The air burned my lungs. My inhales shook, and my shoulders quivered. I closed my eyes and focused on steadying my breath.

"Tell me everything," I finally said. But it was a whisper. The woman's gaze lifted. Her rosy cheeks raised in a small smile, but the sadness hadn't left her eyes. I still didn't know her name. I wasn't sure I wanted to. I didn't know much of anything. And the unknown is terrifying.

"It was last night. Yoav, my husband, and I were walking from our home to my parents for Shabbat. We walked right past here. We saw your van and you lying next to it. It was very cold. And there was blood. We carried you back to Abba's- my dad- he's a doctor."

I shook my head, "You didn't see a dog? Lying right next to me?"

"I really don't remember. We were so concerned about you. But, maybe Yoav remembers."

"Doesn't matter," I whispered, tears brewing again, "he's not here and I don't know where he is."

She knelt down in front of me, in front of the wheelchair.

"Why don't you come back to the house and rest. Tomorrow we will call the tow places and vets and dog pounds," she said. Was it a lure to get me back inside? I looked down at my legs, sitting in a wheelchair. I didn't need to be lured.

"Tomorrow?" I asked, realizing her words. Her eyebrows furrowed.

"We do not make calls on Shabbat." Shabbat...I wasn't sure what that was. A religious holiday maybe?

"What about emergencies?" I asked. This was an emergency.

"This is not an emergency," she quipped and I gaped, "We will call and sort this out, but you need more rest and to get out of this cold." Without another word, she walked around behind me and began to push me forward. I felt frozen. I wanted to jump out of that chair. I wanted to run away. I wanted to climb into my van, with Wolf, and leave this awful town.

So, I gripped the tires and my fingers twisted into the gaps between the metal spokes. She stopped instantly.

"What are you doing?!" she asked.

"I have lost everything. Everything! I'm not going back," and with gritted teeth, I raised myself out of that chair. Then instantly collapsed. My knees buckled under the weight of my hip. A world of pain swirled through my muscles. Cold asphalt met my palms with a sting. My stomach churned and my vision blackened into night.

I felt the woman walk around and kneel beside me. The morning sun invaded the dark until I could see again. The woman's short auburn hair dangled over one of her eyes as she leaned down.

"You have two choices," she said. "Stay here, by yourself, maybe be okay and find your things. Maybe not. Or come with, get warm, heal up, let us help you."

Let us help you.

Sure, let them help me into the trafficking circuit. Let them manipulate me into a victim. Let them help me cave to the groping hands and molestation I'd run so far from. That I'd lost myself in.

I shook my head. I couldn't.

She sighed, long, hard, and shook her head. She looked up with pursed lips.

"Ay, Hashem, what do I do?" she whispered to the swirling clouds. I stared upward, half expecting an answer. But none came. None ever did. The woman smiled and looked back at me. My eyes darted back and forth.

"What?" I asked.

"Don't you hear it?"

I pushed my head forward, trying to hear something. Was God speaking to her and I just couldn't hear it? Was it me? Had God been speaking to me all this time but I was deaf to His voice? I looked down and shook my head.

"I don't hear anything,"

"It's the music of birds. My bubbe always said that no matter where you are, if you can hear the birds singing, there is always hope for tomorrow."

I tilted my head. Somehow I hadn't noticed the chatter of birds. But I could hear them now. Now that I focused on it. Now that I knew what to listen for. And as my ears tuned into the song, the wind whistled along. Riding on the wave of an unseen force, a sliver of cerulean teeter-tottered its way through the metal fence. It hovered, picked up again by the wind and found its resting place on the small oval shaped red stained asphalt.

A feather.

A blue feather.

CHAPTER FIFTEEN

WHEN MEN DON'T TOUCH

It didn't smell like zucchini. I twisted the muffin around on the little pink floral plate. But apparently this is what a zucchini muffin looked like. I ripped a small knob off the top and pushed it through my lips. I didn't feel like eating, but Malka insisted. Right after she wheeled me back inside.

I held my breath as we crossed through the threshold again. Part of me felt crazy for trusting in a bird. What was I returning to? Would Marshall be here, waiting? I couldn't be sure. But if I was going to find Wolf, I couldn't do it on my own. Not with this injury, not in this cold. And someone knew that, whether an angel, God, or a simple little bird.

"Well....?" Malka asked, leaning over the island, chin clasped in her palms, her eyes wide as canyons.

I covered my mouth mid chew, "Good." Then I lifted the floppy empty cupcake paper as evidence.

But she rolled her eyes at me.

"I hope you're not just trying to be polite."

I swallowed, "No, they're very tasty. Really."

Before this point we'd been the only ones in the kitchen or living room area. To my relief. I didn't want to deal with a bunch of strangers. But sooner or later I knew I'd have to, if I were going to be here until tomorrow.

"Oh, feeling better?" A new voice echoed from the hall. Apparently it was sooner. He was old enough for gray hair with a beard that swayed as he walked towards me. I leaned back in the stool, anticipating a hand to grasp my shoulder. None came.

I nodded, but I wasn't sure I actually felt better. The man wore a gentle, tired smile on his face. His gaze crossed over to Malka whose bright grin had dissipated. I swallowed. Why did she seem so sullen all of a sudden? I tugged at the short sleeves that would not reach my wrists. Silence passed for far too long. Was I hearing the sound of our breath moving in and out of our chests in unison?

"This is my abba," Malka said, her eyes smiling more than her lips, "He's a doctor. He fixed your wounds."

"And praise be to Hashem your blood loss was slight enough that we could care for it here. However, I suspect the dressing does need to be changed. Malka?" He turned around and began to walk back down the hall. My eyes flicked to Malka.

"Come, come." She nodded and waved at me to follow her. I stood and gripped the counter as my vision blackened. But it quickly came back. Sunlight danced across the light blue island top. The window above the porcelain sink was framed by thick brown molding, the same as all the windows in the home. Outside, a red brick wall stared back, firm and immovable. Like my feet.

An arm slid beside me and interlaced with mine. Malka.

"Come, it's okay Jay."

I nodded. And at a leaden pace, we went back into the room I'd woken up in.

When I lay down, I was surprised that it was Malka sitting beside me. Her dad stood just behind and to the side.

"I'm going to lift your shirt now, okay?" Malka said softly. My eyes must have read the confusion I was feeling.

"Is that okay?" she asked. My eyes flickered between them both.

"Isn't he the doctor?" I whispered as if only Malka could hear me if I were quiet enough. Malka nodded.

"Malka will be following my instructions," he said, but that didn't really help me.

"It is our custom not to touch the opposite sex," Malka clarified.

Her dad nodded, "There are of course exemptions and impossible situations, but if we are able, we keep separate." Did he do this for all of his female patients? Certainly not, right? And then it hit me. And I felt like I was in the twilight zone. *Men and women don't touch? They don't touch?* My throat started to close. The world was collapsing in on itself.

"You look confused," Malka stated, still waiting to change my dressing.

I pressed my lips together, wondering which part I should reference, "So are you his assistant for the women then?"

She chuckled, "Me? No, my place is at home, baking far too much. Doctors are allowed to touch their patients, which is what Abba does normally," she paused to glance back at him, "It is good for me to learn, and good for Abba to be clean for synagogue."

I nodded, "Okay...I think I get it." She nodded back and lifted the shirt just enough to where my stomach was exposed. Her cold fingers grazed along the outer edge of the bandage at my side.

"I have to move the skirt down just a little," she warned. My eyes flicked up to the spackled ceiling.

"Okay," I said. I tried to not hold my breath as she peeled back the bandage and followed her fathers instructions. They worked in such perfect unison, you'd think they'd done it before.

"There, all set." Malka said with a smile. I looked down at the clean bandage.

"That's it?" I could swear it felt like half a second that had passed.

"Yes, though I am curious about that laceration at your ankle," she said.

I sighed and glanced down at the new bandage, "That was an entirely different situation."

"You seem to get yourself into quite the...situations." Malka said, her voice hanging in expectation of an explanation. It was an odd wound. An even odder story.

"Danger likes to follow me," I finally replied, "I was attacked by a bear a few days ago."

"Mmm," Malka's dad stared at the bandage, assessing files in his mind. Malka's eyes filled with more curiosity and questions, but her mouth didn't open to her wonder. And since they weren't pressing, I too kept quiet. It was better that way. After a while, Malka's dad said something.

"Well," he leaned forward, "the bullet only went through your love handles."

"Which is amazing because you have hardly any fat there!" Malka piqued. I sat up, with a hand over my side. I hadn't really examined it before.

"Yes, blessed indeed." The old man said.

"You mean it's not that bad?" I asked. The abysmal amount

searing torture that I was experiencing in that moment would argue otherwise. Not to mention I could barely get in a breath sitting up like I was.

"No it's not. But you still need your rest." He reminded me with a pointed look at Malka.

"I'll stay here, while everyone heads to synagogue." Malka said.

"Thank you," he turned to the door and left. Mere seconds later another head popped in. Yoav. Malka's husband. I abruptly pulled my shirt all the way over my bandage. This time he was fully clothed in a white button down shirt. A gray jacket sat beneath an oversized black shawl with tassels that danced at his knees.

"Malka, your bubbe doesn't want to come with."

"No?"

"No, she insists on staying."

Malka paused for a moment, "Okay then."

"You're not mad?"

"No, I don't understand. But I'm not mad."

I watched them in silence, seeming to stare at each other, holding a silent language. It was as if they were communicating through thought. Could a person understand another so intimately that there need be no words? Or were they telepathic? I squinted my eyebrows and they both laughed.

CHAPTER SIXTEEN

FEELING EMPTY

Once Yoav and Malka's dad left, I asked to take a shower. One of the downsides to van life was the hassle of getting clean. And I hadn't had a hot one in…months. Of course Malka was more than chipper to oblige, offering me a clean towel and a whole new set of her clothes to borrow. All the while with an absurdly inordinate smile. My stomach churned at the thought of how bad I might reek.

After closing the bathroom door behind me, I tried to take a whiff. I didn't smell anything. Maybe I was immune. I winced thinking back to…to yesterday? With Marshall. How my heart had begun to swoon over a kind man. To be twirled in a hopeful fantasy of romance that never existed. How deeply I desired it. Like a child wishing to go to Disneyland, I wanted to be swept off my feet. I wanted to believe he was prince charming so bad, I made excuses for every red flag.

How could I have been so stupid?! I knew better. And my mistake didn't just hurt me. It hurt Wolf too. The pain of the memory swept my feet out from under me. My back pressed up against the door. My hands shook and I clenched my arms around my knees. My heart ached while my throat burned with acid. My stomach felt as if it were being ripped up through my mouth.

I could barely silence my sobs through my hands. I wanted to scream, but I didn't want a soul to know.

With my body taking jerky inhales, I lifted myself from the floor and turned the shower on. The water fell over me like a curtain. I wanted to drown in that stream. For once in my life I wanted to not feel anything. To go completely numb.

I lifted my arm to smooth my hair from my face and resisted every urge to claw at the dark swirls that plagued my skin. Panic crept in as an unwelcome guest and I had to dig my nails into my palms to keep it at bay. It barely worked. Last thing I wanted right now was to black out in the shower.

I sighed as I reached for the warmth of a towel. Malka was going to have to change my bandage again. I slipped into the foreign garments. *Where had my clothes gone*, I wondered. *Were they destroyed by the bullet...and the blood?*

As the skirt went over my hip, it felt bare, naked without the cold metal appendage and I suddenly felt helpless. Not that it was much help before. I bit my lip and tasted iron as the memories gusted back again.

I opened the bathroom door and peered around the corner. Clear. I hobbled my way to the room across from me. After closing the door, I stood in the center, surveying the room for my weapon, hoping it had somehow been scooped up with me last night - hoping Marshall didn't still have it. I couldn't see it. And my memory kept flashing back to the blast of the shot. The vision of Wolf leaping out in front of me before...before...

He could have kicked Wolf.

He could have had me call him off.

Anything except shoot him!

Tears rolled down my cheeks and my lips quivered. I should have called Wolf. I should have done something, anything.

I should have put myself in the way of him leaping out or I could have even pulled him back. But instead I stood there like an idiot. Terrified. My terror...I couldn't even think what it caused him. *And where was he? Where was my dog?!*

I picked up a pillow and slammed it against the bed. I had no control. I was utterly and entirely trapped. My face grew hot. Voices echoed from another room. My mind guessed it was about me, but I couldn't be sure. Couldn't care. I wanted out.

But I was anchored to this nightmare. My head felt swollen and the bridge of my nose hurt from crying. I needed to do something...but what? Light filled the room, bouncing off the white sparkling snow that was fading away outside. Erasing the blizzard of last night. If only it could erase everything from that night.

I walked to the window and pressed my forehead against the cold glass. With closed eyes, I tried to imagine a good scenario in my head. An explanation of Wolf's disappearance. I walked it all out in my mind, searching for clues.

Wolf jumped, I leaped. Gunshot. On the ground. Marshall over us. Pain and blood. The whine of Wolf just barely out of my reach. What was it Marshall had said? I pressed my forehead harder into the glass as if frigid hard pressure might pull clarity into the memory.

Marshall....he said he was going to get help. *Help. From where?* Malka and her husband must have come by after he left. I turned away from the window. It just didn't make sense. Wolf had to have been there, but they didn't notice him?

I stared at the brown carpet but didn't see it, I was remembering the blood and the white fur...next to me. Close. But maybe not as close as I thought. *Maybe Marshall came back but*

I was gone. He had Wolf. He had bait and an advantage.

I looked up. Fury filled my veins. I wanted to scream as my vision blurred into a murky haze. I clenched my jaw so hard I felt a pop near my right ear. My chest heaved, and I blinked away the fog. But the darkness remained. I knew what I needed to do.

I needed my gun.

CHAPTER SEVENTEEN
MARKS OF INHUMANITY

I swung open the door so fast that I almost ran into it, my baby hairs flying backwards like the wings of a hawk. The rest of my still wet hair dripped down the front of Malka's black velvet top. I needed to know if I'd had my gun on me, if they grabbed it when they grabbed me. I had no idea what I was about to face, what kind of protests I might have to battle.

And I had no idea what I'd do if my gun was as lost as my dog. I tried to remember what happened to it. A large part of me felt like I remembered him setting it beside me before running off - but that made no sense. It was probably no use. Marshall had my gun. As much as I hated the thought, I was going to have to steal a knife from this family. What other option did I have?

With a large inhale, I set out into the hallway and followed the voices down the corridor. There were more than two, melting and weaving, bubbling over each other in a chaotic chorus I couldn't understand. It had been a long time since I put myself around people and as I stepped into the living room, three sets of eyes scanned to me. The voices stopped.

I stood, frozen. My own voice caught in my throat. Every bit of bravery I had a second ago had been emptied from my deflated corpse. I attempted a smile, but my cheeks felt like two glaciers pushing into each other.

Thankfully, I didn't have to wait long.

"Jay!" Malka beamed in her bright blue dress and waved me over, sensing my obvious awkward entry. I moved my feet forward and gripped the ends of my sleeves, thankful this top reached to my wrists.

There were two other women in the room, sitting side by side on a brown leather couch against the window by the door. They all had similar cheeks and noses that curved towards their top lip, much like an overhang I once attempted to climb. I knew, before Malka could tell me, that they were related.

"Jay, this is Mama and Bubbe." She said, pointing to each woman respectively. They both smiled, more so with their eyes than their mouths. The expressions on their faces yelled that questions were charging through their minds. Malka tapped the open seat next to her on the adjacent love seat.

"You may call me Mayim," Malka's mother said. She was dressed in all black and her thin lips were held taught. I took no time to sit, the pain in my hip increasing the longer I stood. The cream love seat was soft and I nearly disappeared into it.

"My name is Martha, but feel free to call me Bubbe," she whispered to me with a smile. Her eyes sparkled behind silver rimmed glasses. She too was in a long skirt and a red fabric graced her head. Even though I shared the loveseat with Malka, I was closer to the older woman on the adjacent couch.

"What on earth is a young girl doing out at night all on her own?" Immediately Mayim's voice cut through the air, her eyebrows arched in opposite directions.

"So quick to judge, as always." Bubbe snapped at her. Malka laughed. I wanted to crawl out of my skin. I kept away from people for a reason.

"I was not judging. Only asking. Is it not a worthwhile question?" She retorted. The grandmother snorted in response and I sensed they bickered like this regularly. My unease gurgled the acid in my stomach.

"It's true," Malka said, "we are curious about what happened."

"But it's not nice to pry." Bubbe said, looking at both of them with raised eyebrows.

I couldn't help smiling. And they all noticed. It was perhaps the first moment the ice melted from my face. I was no longer as stoic. No longer granite. Maybe I could get through this. Maybe I could interact with people. But now they were all staring. The smile slipped into a straight line and it suddenly felt like a vice was pressing on my chest.

"I wasn't alone." I finally said.

"Yes, Malka mentioned you had a dog?" Mayim questioned, her face softer than before. I blinked several times and cleared my throat, hoping that talking about him wouldn't break me into hysterics. They didn't need to see that and I certainly didn't need to lose control again.

"Yeah. He was protecting me. And the guy sh… shot him." I focused on my breath, pushing it out slowly as I mentally screamed at the tears that wanted to break free. An uneasy feeling settled in the room, like gas pressing from all around. Malka's gaze dropped and Mayim leaned back in the sofa, seemingly resolved.

"It is dangerous out there," Mayim said, her eyebrows still down, crowding out the green color of her irises.

"So you were attacked? What happened after he shot you?" Malka asked, her voice higher than before. I put my face into my hand and rubbed my forehead. I didn't want to go over it. I couldn't. But like everything else, I shoved last night into some cavern within me.

"No, I wasn't," I whispered.

"You weren't what dear?" Bubbe asked as she reached out to rub the side of my arm. Without thinking about it, I shifted out of the way of her graze. I looked up, to apologize, but her eyes glistened. As if tears were beginning to brew. I caused that. She held up her hand, halting my need to say sorry. I shook my head and remembered her question.

"I wasn't attacked." I muttered. The crunch of the leather couch made me glance up. Malka flicked at one of the large heart shaped dangle earrings she was wearing. Why was talking so hard? My voice didn't want to exit my mouth. The wind of my vocals were snared in the depths of my throat.

The three women waited, eager, yet patient. I blew out the wind and began to string together more than enough words for just one sentence.

"I was panicking," I verbally admitted as my face grew hotter. How much should I admit to? Were my feet already too deep in sinking sand? I tried to word it in my head first, to make it sound right - sound okay. *I thought he was going to kidnap me and force me into sex trafficking, my dog sensed my panic and went after him.*

But instead, "I thought he was going to take me back home."

Everyone leaned forward. *Great*, I thought, *I blew that one*, how on earth was I going to explain that? But before I could say a word, Mayim stood, her black bob as blunt as her. I shrunk back in my seat. My stomach felt like dust floating above a misty cove. And had her gaze not turned away so quickly, I might have hurled right then and there.

"I think we need food, Malka." Mayim tipped her head to the

side and Malka stood. Our eyes met and I tried to understand the thoughts pouring through her down turned lashes. But no words, no smile, no shrug, no hint at anything. I felt like I was on a continual roller coaster trying to figure these people out. Maybe it would be easier if I could communicate like a normal person.

But I was far from normal. Normality was stricken from me. Pulled out like a weed in a beautiful garden, left to shrivel up and die in the sun. And my garden now was nothing more than a desert; bare, empty, and lonely. Wolf was my succulent, and that too was gone.

"What do you like to do for fun?" Bubbe chimed over my wandering thoughts, her voice bubbly and shaky all at once. Like the vibration of a waterfall, hard to comprehend but altogether breathtaking.

"Um," I gulped, a little taken aback, "I like to rock climb," I offered. She smiled and I did too. She looked up towards the speckled ceiling. I thought for a moment she might start talking to God like Malka had. I couldn't quite decide If I wanted her to or not. God and I were not on the best of terms.

"Yes, climbing to overcome your past and reach Hashem." She smiled at me, again. I furrowed my eyebrows. What on earth was she talking about? She pointed her arm towards the coffee table between us and that's when I saw it. I couldn't help it. The tears bubbled up, fogging up the view of what she was trying to show me. But all I could see were the marks on her arm. The branding. The numbers of a beast.

She was a holocaust survivor.

I did everything to hide mine. But she brazenly displayed hers. There was no tugging at her sleeves. No effort to hide who she was or the past she endured. I wanted to ask how.

How could she be so open with it? So unafraid. I thought of my own tattoo, a curly C with a dollar sign in the middle, and felt sick.

It was my parents business card, a signal to the sick bastards who could recognize it whenever we went out. And I was rarely allowed to cover it. Now that I'd escaped, I'd contemplated cutting it off multiple times, but ultimately reneged on the thought. I was saving up for a cover tattoo, but I had no idea what image to replace it with. I suppose anything would be better.

Maybe a blue jay...in watercolor - for all the tears I've cried.

I was like livestock, branded for one specific use - and just as easy to discard. It made me sick. I wanted to scratch away the skin of my arm but settled for pulling at the sleeve.

At the end of Bubbe's finger was a black and white picture. It was a young woman, grinning so hard it made me happy, skating on ice as snow fluttered around her.

"You have to find it," she said, "The thing Hashem has given you joy in. Heartache and hard times will always be. When the light shines, hold on to it, because darkness always returns." I stared, mouth hanging partially open at this woman whose words sounded like something out of science fiction - or a self help book. I shut my mouth when Malka and her mother started making their way back to the sofa from the kitchen. Mayim had drinks in her hand and Malka had a cheese and cracker tray.

"Well, what's wrong with home?" Mayim asked without hesitation - before even sitting back down as if she had never left from the conversation. I brushed my damp hair aside. Malka's eyes were wide with anticipation. Or fear. Or maybe curiosity? I wasn't sure. Mayim's eyebrows were down, waiting for a response. I glanced over to Bubbe who was too involved in picking out one of the many different sorts of cheese. Some of which I wouldn't dare attempt to even pronounce.

Mayim cleared her throat. I swung my head back at her. "Um…" How much did I say? What would this close knit family think of a girl who was tainted? Ruined? Used? I'd been sexual with more men than either Malka or Mayim had ever even touched. Surely they'd be disgusted. And throw me out. And I still didn't have my gun.

I closed my eyes, "My parents…were abusive. I ran away when I was 18."

"Not sooner?" Mayim asked, her eyes wide.

"Mama!" Malka shouted

"It's a reasonable question. Who knows, these days kids think a parent raising their voice is abuse." She shrugged her shoulders. Bubbe seemed to have sunk away from the conversation entirely as she nibbled on her snack. I could use her rescuing again, but it wasn't coming. I'd have to face Mayim's brazen accusations on my own.

I took a deep breath, "They forced me into prostitution and beat me if I didn't comply," I stated with shaking hands. It was the first time I ever said that out loud. The first time I told anyone since that Sunday at church.

The first time I didn't keep it a secret.

Tears started rolling down my cheeks and I couldn't see clearly enough to know what their expressions said. I wasn't sure I wanted to know. If I didn't leave the room, I might have burst. Though I winced standing up, and altogether wanted to scream, I forced myself away from the couches and into the hall.

But I couldn't breathe any better there. The fog of cinnamon swirled through the air. Even if it was only in my mind. Vanilla danced like a taunting spirit around me.

Footsteps followed, pit patting across the carpet.

Faster, almost to me.

The hallway narrowed.

My chest tightened and my head felt empty. Bile rolled up my esophagus. The hallway spun and oozed and meshed together in a kaleidoscope of earth tones. I swore I could feel someone's hand reach around my throat. I grasped for the wall but darkness consumed me.

CHAPTER EIGHTEEN

LOST TIME

W hite powder covered my palms. Years of climbing created caverns and calluses. I shook my hands and clapped them together, puffing a chalk cloud into the air. I reached for a hold and found a man-made crevice. I stepped onto the wall, making sure I was tight against it. One hold at a time. The farther up I went, the softer the voices below became. I looked up from my hold to see how close I was to the top.

I gasped. Instead of a stark white ceiling, the blue sky danced above my head, broken only by streaks of thin cirrus clouds. I pulled my body forward and peeked over my shoulder. My foot slipped, and pebbles tumbled to the abyss below. I gripped tighter onto my hand holds. I must have been thirty feet up. I shut my eyes and grit my teeth. What was happening?!

"Bridget," a voice whispered. My spine tingled. Something was crawling up my thigh. I didn't want to look. But my desire to ignore the fingers creeping over my skin didn't stop it.

"Bridget," again the whisper came. One, two, three. I opened my eyes. I could still feel the rock beneath my hands, and the emptiness below. Yet somehow there was a floor under my feet. Brightly colored shag carpet, deceptively rough. A large hand sat on my thigh, a thigh too small to be my own.

"Bridget," said the man, whose face hovered in front of me as his hand slid over my shorts and rested at the silver button that held them closed.

He smiled, "Now it's your turn to feel good."

"No," I whispered.

"What?" he asked.

"No," I clarified. He tilted his head.

"NO!"

My eyes shot open to an entirely different world. The vibration of my heart in my chest slowed as I surveyed the room. I wasn't on carpet. I was on a bed. A rectangle of yellow glowed on the wall. I sighed. I was in the real world, in a real room, a familiar one. I was in Malka's home. My head hurt. I squeezed my eyes shut trying to remember the events that took me there. I reached up to my neck, remembering the hand I'd felt.

"Jay?" A soft voice asked from the door. A woman stood there in a long baby blue robe. Her hair was red, falling in waves to her hips. Her face held concern. I rubbed my eyes, entirely confused at what I was seeing. It looked like Malka, but Malka had short brown hair.

"Yeah?" I said finally, not entirely convinced of who I was speaking to. She slipped inside and gently shut the door behind her.

"I thought I heard you shouting." She said, and I bit my lip, not wanting to get into the nightmare I just had.

"I was worried." She said, "You seemed to have fainted. But you've been asleep for a really long time. We took you in here and checked your wound again. I didn't see any sign of infection and I wasn't sure what happened and if we caused it-"

"Malka?" I interrupted, squinting at her.

"Yes?" She looked at me.

"How long have I been asleep?" My heart rate started picking up again. Was that why her hair was different? Instantly I thought of Wolf and all my hopes were gone. My best friend. He was there for me. Constantly by my side. He protected me and I couldn't be there for him. My mind raced and my fingers gripped the blanket laying over me. I could feel the heat rise in my eyes and puddles form into lakes. Wolf was gone. My breathing got deeper. I swallowed heavily and the world started to spin again.

"About five hours," she said. I closed my eyes and bowed my head into my knees. My body shook and I didn't even attempt to hide that I was sobbing. My emotions spilled out as relief flooded me. And then I started to laugh. When I looked up, Malka was staring.

"Are you okay?" she asked. No, I wasn't. But I wasn't going to admit that.

"Yes," I sighed and swung my legs over the side of the bed. Malka sat down next to me and I realized she'd been holding a yellow mug in her hands this entire time.

"I have this thing," I began, "where my body shuts down in intense situations often caused by my own anxiety."

"Sounds rough," her eyes were wide, absorbing the information, "and dangerous."

"I usually don't black out. I've been working on controlling my emotions…it's better…when I'm alone."

"I see." She said in a quiet voice and I suddenly hoped she didn't take it the wrong way.

"Malka?" I asked, changing the subject and addressing my curiosity.

"Uh huh?"

"What happened to your hair?" I asked and she flung her hand to her head with worried eyes. And then they softened and she chuckled.

"Oh," she walked out of the room and I sat up. Was she coming back?

Malka popped in with something dark dangling from her hand. Hair.

"No way," I gaped.

"It's tradition to veil our hair." She said, sitting down again.

"Can I see?" she handed it over to me as I examined it.

"It's so realistic," I whispered.

"I should hope so, it wasn't cheap." She laughed and I smiled. But the softness of the hair in my hands sent me back in time and reminded me of Wolf. I quickly gave it back and tugged at my sleeves. I needed to find him. This wasn't right. It wasn't okay. I didn't even know if he was still alive all the while I was sitting there safe, laughing. Images of crimson flooded my mind and I held in a scream.

Malka took my hand but I didn't flinch.

And I remembered the feather.

"One day at a time," she said. I wasn't confident that I had a day. I wasn't confident of anything. Even now, feeling the warmth and comfort flowing out from Malka's presence, a part of me wondered if it was all demure. A facade I allowed myself to believe. Maybe if I accepted the disappointment and betrayal now, it wouldn't hurt so much when it came.

"One day at a time," I repeated, squeezing her hand back.

"You must be hungry," Malka said, "Come, mama made Tzimmes and hers is the best in the whole block."

"What's Tzimmes?" I asked as she yanked me out of the bed

while somehow not spilling an ounce of her tea.

She paused at the door, "A sweet stew, you'll love it! You'd have to be crazy not to."

I smiled wryly, "Okay."

"Come on," she insisted.

"I'm coming, I'm coming," I said as I followed her down the hall. I didn't really want to go back out there. A weird feeling twisted in my abdomen, but it wasn't nerves. I liked Malka. That realization nearly caused me to trip as we rounded into the kitchen. To my relief, no one else was there.

Malka lifted the lid of a crockpot and steam swirled into the air.

"Still warm," she grinned and set the lid on the counter.

"Ah! She's up!" a soft male voice sounded from behind me. I froze. We weren't all alone. I turned, vaguely recognizing the voice.

"I'm alive," I said to Yoav as he took a seat at the island.

A steaming bowl of stew was pushed in front of me. I decided to stand while I scooped up a spoon of carrots and raisins.

"Mmmm Tzimmes! You'll love it," he said.

"So I hear," I mumbled before consuming the spoonful. Malka and Yoav gazed expectantly - almost holding their breath even. It was sweet and satisfying, like a warm mug of tea. The raisins were an unexpected, yet pleasant texture. And I normally couldn't care for raisins.

"This is good," I nodded with another spoonful. I was famished.

"She usually only cooks it for Rosh Hashanah, but-"

Yoav interrupted Malka, "She swore up and down that this shabbat would be special."

"And," Malka beamed, "she was right, yet again." I eyed both of them.

"What do you mean?" I asked between bites. Malka twirled her mug and took a sip.

Yoav leaned into his palm, "The last time she had a feeling of something was the day we told her you were pregnant."

"Mama always knows," Malka said.

My spoon clinked against the side of the bowl, "So something special happened again?"

"Don't be silly," Malka exclaimed, "Of course!"

"She means you," Yoav chuckled as confusion twisted over my face.

"Me?" But how could I be anything special? I was nobody. I was a stranger. And I'd done nothing for this family.

"But Mayim was sooo…"

"Hostile?" Yoav asked

Malka laughed, "That's just mama, you should have seen her with poor Yoav our first year of marriage."

Yoav wiped his brow and snickered as his cheeks flushed bright red. I nodded, beginning to understand, but feeling far away from comprehending the depth this family seemed to hold. I once naively imagined a life like theirs. But it'd been so long since I contemplated marriage, even a boyfriend, or the absurd idea of a large family unit. As if my parents would ever allow such a thing. As if I'd ever be okay with a man that was okay with what my parents did.

All I had was Wolf and I was happy with that. Tomorrow I was going to find him. And if I found Marshall too, I might just kill him.

CHAPTER NINETEEN

WHAT ONCE WAS LOST IS NOW FOUND

The anticipation of a voice on the other end of the phone held me captive. The pen in my hand felt as cold as my bare feet on the tile. I bit the inside of my cheek as the sound of a woman echoed on the other end, welcoming me to purpose my question. I handed it over like vomit.

I waited while she searched her database for an injured husky. Instead of the encouragement my heart ached for, I was met with a solemn apology. I hung up the phone and dialed the next possibility. But hope was dry ice melting, whose fog dissipated quickly. There were only two veterinary clinics near the area. The others were possible, but it was doubtful he'd be there. They were a half hour away. If he wasn't at a vet, my next shot would be the pounds. But I'd suppose that even if a pound picked up an injured dog, they'd send him to the vet...or leave him in the cold. Beyond that I had no option, nothing other than a posted paper of a lost dog. But if those rarely worked for humans...what good could they do for an animal?

The last place I'd seen Wolf and Marshall was in that parking lot. If this failed, I'd wait there. If Marshall had Wolf as bait, he'd be sure to show up at the lot.

My heart started as a voice echoed in my ear. I stammered off a request for my best friend. A husky with a possible gunshot wound. I felt my eyebrows connect as I uttered the injury.

"Oh yes! Such a sweet boy!" she said instantly. I nearly dropped the phone and collapsed to the floor. Tears flooded my eyes as I let out an exhale.

"I was there when he brought him in, poor guy," she continued. "I'm sure he'll be happy to go home."

"Is he okay?" was all I could barely utter through a rattled voice.

"He's got a limp, but he's clear to go. The vet can go over all the details when you get here."

I covered my mouth and closed my eyes.

"Thank you," I said. The phone fell like a paper weight from my hands. Through the tiny kitchen window, rays of morning light glimmered off brick. A tree with barely any leaves danced in celebration.

Hearing someone come up behind me, I turned, hoping to see Malka and share my excitement. Instead, I was met with the deep set eyes of her mother. The last we spoke, I had run off. What sort of judgment was going to pour out of her mouth this time. What poison apple would I have to consume? And would it be the death of me? Was I going to fall into another temporary coma?

But worse than saying something, she pushed her lips closed and walked around me to grab a mug out of the cupboard. The pour of hot coffee into her cup seemed louder than was possible. And I couldn't speak over it.

"I'm sorry," I started when she reached for the fridge, "I

shouldn't have run off the way I did."

She glanced at me and for a moment I thought she might say something. Rather, she closed her mouth and opened the fridge door. I'd never seen such pristine organization. Every shelf was lined with clear containers, all labeled with a cursive note of what was inside and a date. I wanted to try again, attempt to make amends but the lump in my throat was making that impossible.

In my small window of happiness, I felt crushed again. But what was I expecting? What could I ever expect? My past twisted me into this ugly creature. I could never live up to their standards.

I wondered who else felt the same way as Mayim. Everyone else seemed about as kind as Malka, but I didn't really know them and by now they had all heard of my past. They must want me out of their house as soon as possible.

I turned away from Mayim as she sipped on her coffee and stared out the kitchen window. I needed to find my van and get out of here. I glanced down at the numbers I had compiled of possible places it might have been taken and quickly pressed out the first one.

Nearly an hour later and after many roundabout redirections, I'd found it. It had in fact been taken to the impound yard. I stretched my legs under the table where I'd relocated to. Each person had moved in and out of the kitchen in that time, smiling and nodding at me as they went. I tried not to think about the truth hidden behind their smiles. But it ate away at me in the back of my mind.

Worst of all was probably Mayim sitting in the chair next to me the entire time. I watched her read a book and then pull out a light blue box of stationary and write letters, never once even glancing at me. Every time I had to speak, I felt nervous, like I might be disrupting her space. Yet the longer it went on, I felt as if I might've well been an inanimate object. Was it that bad? That she didn't want to acknowledge my existence? Perhaps that was how she was coping with what I told her. Just ignoring it completely. Like everyone else in my life.

"Did you find what you were searching for?" her voice broke through the silence. My eyes darted over to her sitting back in the white wood chair, hands folded in her lap with all her stationary tucked away.

"Yes," I nodded and scooted my seat out with a screech loud enough to make us both wince.

"Sit," she commanded. I blinked, feeling uneasy with the command. I shot a glance down the hallway, hoping for Malka.

Mayim swatted the air, "No need for panic," she said and forced a smile. I swallowed, wondering what was going to happen. What on earth was on this woman's mind? I dug my nails into the palms of my hands, surprised by how long I'd let them get.

"Now," she began, "I am sorry, these words of mine aren't so easily controlled." She sighed and I raised an eyebrow, having witnessed over an hour of her ignorance and held silence.

"I know the way we live here is not like the rest of the world. I am not naive. Many of us have our own problems we must face and a lot of what we do is to combat situations like yours where lust is out of hand. But even so, it is not always enough." She sighed. I leaned back.

Mayim continued, "I'm a bit harsh, only because I know the reality of sin. Of what it does to people, to families. And I hate it. Even more than custard-which is vile." She said with a little laugh. I smiled. It was refreshing to see her seriousness fade away.

"Anyways," she said, "I must stop myself before I unload all our community problems on you. I hope you'll forgive this woman." She pointed to herself and I didn't know what to say.

"Thank you," I mustered up and paused, her words still swirling through my mind, pricking the fabric of who I'd assumed her to be.

"I forgive you." I said finally, "I'm not good with people."

"Then we are not so different." She said and stood. She smiled with her chest out. I pinned my lips together and she turned down the hall, where Yoav glided around the corner. I clenched my sleeves.

His dark figure was coming my way. I wanted to get up and go, but also didn't want to pass by him in the hall. So I waited. He stopped at the table, looking at me.

I held my head back in anticipation. What was going on here?

"Malka has asked for me to come get you," he said so quietly and softly I barely understood him. I stood, and then had to grab hold of the table as my knee wobbled out from under me.

"Are you okay?" he asked, not even flinching to brace me. I looked up at him from under my hair.

"Yeah…I think," I took a hesitant step away from the table. Tingles were raging up my entire right leg before turning into thumbtacks sinking into my flesh. I nodded at Yoav and followed him down the hall. Another mystery. Why did Malka have to send Yoav to get me?

He stood by the door of the room I'd been staying in the last couple days. I held my breath as he turned the knob. This felt odd. He smiled at me, different than Mayim had been smiling at me only moments ago. This was happier.

Behind the door stood Malka in the center of the room. She was biting her lower lip. In a second, she then jumped to the side. Behind her was a circular table that I didn't remember being there before. On the table in the center was a giant basket with an oversized white ribbon at the base of the handle. I looked at it and over at Malka's beaming face, then back at it.

"Surprise!" Malka said as I gathered myself and approached the table. My eyes watered, looking everything over. My hands felt along the ribbed rim. In the back were several pieces of clothing. Next were some bath goodies, a journal with a blue pen, a little book with 'The Torah' on the cover, and a bag of Malka's muffins I'd swore were completely eaten up last night. And a little blue card. Mayim must have snuck it in after leaving the table.

"Why are you so kind?" I asked.

Malka shrugged, "Why not?"

"You don't even know me," I said.

"You don't need to know someone to show them HaShem," Yoav's low voice sounded behind me.

"Come come, there's more."

"What?" I asked but Malka was already shuffling out the door. I looked at Yoav, who waited for me. I followed farther down the hall, a part of the home I hadn't been in. Besides the bathroom, there were three other rooms. Malka entered the second one to the end.

I hesitated for a second, my mind instantly going to dark places, speculating a trap. Even when logic said it didn't make sense. I rubbed my sleeves.

When I entered, it didn't seem like anything special, but Bubbe was sitting on the bed, beaming in her yellow floral top. She patted the bed next to her. Malka sat on her knees on the floor as I sunk into the mattress.

"I hear you are leaving us soon," she said.

"Yes, I found my van and dog," I replied. Then I heard a smack. I looked over at Malka whose hand was stuck to her face.

"I did not even ask if you found him. I just heard it from mama. I'm so sorry Jay. I'm so happy for you."

"It's okay," I smiled down at her.

"Well," Bubbe said, "I want you to have this," and she lifted a delicate silver necklace from her hands. Dangling from the silver chain was a small baby blue stone tucked into a silver case. I blinked and held out my hand.

"Oh, but if you don't mind," she said with a nod to my neck. I shook my head and turned around, unable to form any proper words. Her hands shook as she wrapped them around and behind to clasp it. When I turned back around, she was the one with tears.

"It was meant for you," she said and I gazed down at it, as much as I could see, holding the cool stone in my hand.

"Thank you, you all really didn't have to do all this," I said, beginning to wonder about the cost.

"Bubbe, you must tell her the story." Malka pipped.

"I was getting to that my dear," she said.

"What story?" I asked.

"The story of that necklace."

PART TWO

OUT

CHAPTER TWENTY

BLUE SKY

I pulled my legs up onto the bed, eager to hear the backstory of the jewelry around my neck. They looked at it in awe, looked at it *on me* in awe, and I had to shift in the bed again.

"I was ten years old," Bubbe began, "When my mother, brother, and I entered the first camp. My brother was only one. They were killed in the gas chambers that day but I was separated from them and spent seven years surviving." She took a pause and then continued with glossy eyes.

"Many people have told me I was one of the lucky ones. To not die. To survive multiple cases of disease. To go on, even when my body was too thin and too weak with no nutrition. To stay sane seeing death daily, understanding the depths of true horror. But I disagree. Had I been lucky, I'd have died that day with my mother and brother." She paused as I breathed into my fists. It was hard to hear, hard to grasp, even when I personally knew how cruel people could be.

"Many understood that it was better to die and be at peace. So many had nothing to hold on to. They were crushed, mind, body, and soul. But I had something to hold on to. And what I had could not be so easily stamped out." A few tears rolled down her rosy cheeks as she recounted.

"I was outside, with the other girls who had gotten their periods. We were being led to a transfer truck to go to a different camp. We all believed we were going to die that day. I'll never forget walking to that truck." she paused, pursed her lips and caught my eyes, "I heard a voice in my head tell me, 'look up'. At first I thought it might have been a guard but they were all stoic, silent and ashen faced. So I looked up. It was as if I'd been living in black and white my whole life. And seeing that bright blue sky was like living in roaring color. Something about it gave me such a surge in my heart." Bubbe cleared her throat.

"So everyday forward, I looked up. Most days the sky was gray, but I held on for a chance to look up. To see the blue, to feel that surge. I never heard the voice again, but I think about it all the time. Without it, I would have given up. So the first thing I bought myself when I had my own money, was this necklace. It reminded me of the blue sky, and the delicacy of which my life hung." My hand shot to the necklace and my mouth hung open. The necklace suddenly felt too heavy. I wasn't deserving of the emblem I wore. I shook my head. Why on earth was she giving me something so precious? Shouldn't Malka be the one to inherit it?

"You need it much more than I do anymore," she said as if I'd said it out loud, "HaShem has blessed me beyond measure, given me a life I could never have imagined. I surely thought I'd been robbed of ever having children. I am doubled over in hope and happiness. I see so much pain in your eyes. There is always hope. And when you forget it, just look up, look for the blue bits."

"I don't even know what to say," I whispered, "Thank you,"

Bubbe smiled with a glimmer in her eyes. I turned the necklace in my fingers, my heart twisted in a way I didn't understand. How could I ever repay them for their kindness?

"Well, now that everyone is crying, let's give this girl some food before she must go" Malka's father echoed from the doorway. I turned to look at him and Mayim stood next to him, all pink eyed.

The car hummed while I hesitated. Part of me didn't want to leave them and end what felt like a pause in the chaos of my life. But I knew that if I didn't go, the sweet solace would turn sour. As it always does. So I opened the door and stepped out.

"Are you sure you're okay?" Malka asked, leaning over the center console.

"Yes, I'm sure. I have to do this on my own." I insisted. She gave a thin smile.

"Okay, but call us if you need any help."

"Okay," I promised.

"Jay, I mean it. The number is on the card mama wrote."

I bit my cheek and took a mental note "Okay, well, I better go."

"When you're settled, call. We're friends now, keep it that

way."

"I don't have a phone," I reminded her.

"Then write a letter!" she yelled before pulling away. I sighed and spun around to the building behind me, wincing at the slight sting from my hip. I couldn't believe how empty I felt standing alone again.

The building was a bland cream with black glass doors. I reached for the handle with my left hand, holding the gift basket in my right, feeling the cold metal of my revolver tucked into my freshly washed jeans. Malka didn't question me about the gun when she handed it back. And I didn't explain. I was in too much shock. I still couldn't figure out how the revolver ended up with me. Malka said it was laying by my hand when they found me that night. But I still couldn't understand why he'd leave it. Maybe he was in too much of a panic, losing the thing he was supposed to take back. I was no good to them dead.

A giant puff of air blasted me as I walked in, as if it wasn't already cold enough. A man with a deep set tan and short black hair lifted his head from behind a glass wall.

"Can I help you?" he asked.

"I hope so," I said, "I'm looking for my dark blue box van. I called this morning and they said it was here."

He took a moment, clicking on his computer.

"Jay?"

"Yep."

"Okay, we just need ID and a hundred dollars," He said. I took a sharp inhale. I had neither. He glanced up at me with blank eyes.

"Uhhh...I don't have my ID or any money."

"Library card, birth certificate, Social security card. Any of those will work, but you would still need to pay the fine."

I blinked and racked my brain.

"Wait, I have those things…they're just, they're in the van." I offered and he narrowed his eyes at me, as if I might be pulling a fast one.

"I'm serious, I live out of my van, everything is in there. If you just let me get in my van, I can get those things." I flicked my fingernails on the basket handle as I waited for him to mentally process my request.

Finally, "Okay, I'll meet you around the side of the building here." He said and pointed out the door.

"Thank you so much!" I said. He led me out to the lot, full of every sort of vehicle, type and color. The gravel crunched as we walked down the row. I could already spot my van. I imagined Wolf's head popping up at the window like he always did, but I knew that was an impossibility. My nose burned. If I could get through this quickly enough, I could go see him. My pace spurred into an almost run and I was the one leading the way.

My hand shot for the door and swung it open, thankful it wasn't locked. I didn't have the keys on me either. I nearly fell backwards as I took in the state of my van.

"This is how it was when we picked it up," he said. I shuffled away from him, standing a little too close for my comfort. I shook my head.

"No," I whispered as I climbed inside. The floor was covered in trash, my shelves empty. Even the bedding was stripped. I opened the mini cupboard and the drawers under the bed. All empty.

Panic gave way as I dove into the front seat and stuck my hand in between the center console and the seat. I strained to reach them, biting my cheek as the pressure pinched my hand. I let out my breath as my finger latched onto my keys.

I went to put the key into the dashboard and felt like everything was going to fall out under me when I realized it wasn't locked and the papers all over the floor were the torn up manual that was kept in that compartment. I opened the dashboard anyway. Sure enough, my documents were gone.

I slumped back and put my head in my hands. I tried to steady my breath, but my entire body was shaking. I wanted to crumple up, throw up my hands and give in. But I climbed into the back. I shot a glance at the counter where I'd placed the wallets. Empty.

I took one last deep breath and lifted the mattress. The five hundred dollars I had stashed for emergencies was obviously not hidden well enough. I looked over at the man with a lump in my throat.

"I…I don't have anything." As each second ticked, my breathing became more erratic. The implications of this? Could destroy me. A little voice in me wondered if this was Marshall. I pushed the thought away. I didn't need to be worrying about worst case scenarios in an already worst case.

"I'm sorry. If you can get the fee, I'll let you drive her off the lot," he said.

"How am I supposed to do that? Everything is gone. They took *everything* from me."

"Do you have a bank you can go into? They'd hand you the cash. Might be a good idea to have your card closed while you're there." He leaned against the opening as if this could so easily be solved.

I laughed, "No. No I don't. Ugh! Why?! No, my bank is completely online."

He sighed and was silent for a moment before he grinned. My heart beat faster as dread settled in my stomach. I knew that look. *Fuck.*

"Tell you what, I'll let you pay the fee another way," he said and I'm sure he thought he was a knight in shining armor. I wanted to kick him in the jaw. But instead I stood there gaping at him.

"Are you kidding me?!" I screamed. He backed away from me with a smirk still plastered on his face.

"Well it's that or you can go through all the hassle to get your van back. You have thirty days and then it's ours." His eyes knew he had me. He saw an opportunity and seized it. I clenched my fists and grit my teeth. The last person I was intimate with wasn't by choice, and I swore I'd never let that happen again.

I almost told him that even if he wasn't blackmailing me, I'd never be with someone like him. But I took a glance at the empty parking lot. My knees felt week, imagining how easily he could overpower me and shut us in the van.

"Thank you, but I'll find a way to come up with the money and paperwork." I uttered as kindly as I could muster. His eyes narrowed but he let me pass out of the van. His cologne made my stomach dip as I did. His footsteps were step for step behind me. I swallowed and focused on the street in front of me. *Please God, don't let him grab me.*

I passed the main building and glanced backwards. He was gone. I sighed and crossed my arms as I stared into the street, remembering I'd had my gun on me the whole time. I wasn't a helpless victim.

"Shit." I muttered. I left the basket in the van. I squinted at the blue rectangle, halfway hidden behind a silver nissan. I almost considered going back and threatening the man with my gun, but that wasn't me. I'd use it if I had to - if I was being attacked.

A faint mixture of gas and rubber permeated the air as I moved to the sidewalk. I looked up but the sky was gray. Solid gray, like one giant sheet of a cloud that hung over my life. I felt for the folded paper in my pocket that had the name and address of the vet.

Only I had no idea how to reach that address without a map…without my laptop telling me. And when I did get there, would they allow me to take Wolf without paying?

Yep, my momentary peaceful bubble had popped.

CHAPTER TWENTY-ONE

COMPLACENT MINDS

After asking five random strangers for directions, I found my way to the vet. My feet and my side were aching but my ankle had finally healed up enough to no longer be sore. At this point, I needed to find the positives where I could. They were few and far in between. Maybe if I focused enough on the good, I could attract more. I needed every shred I could take. I needed Wolf.

I took a pause at a black metal bench, halfway between dread and excitement for what I was going to face behind those doors. The sun shined off the neon green building like a beacon of hope.

The leaves rustled behind me. I glanced to see two tiny brown birds hopping through the grass before flying off. The sound of barks echoed in the distance. I closed my eyes, pulled my sleeves as far over my hands as I could and started towards the entrance. My arms felt about as strong as jello as I pulled the door open. A tropical air freshener barely masked the thick stench of animals and urine.

"Hi, welcome to Pets Plaze, we'll be right with you!" A woman with black braids smiled up at me. I nodded and rubbed my hands together. I was doing my best to hold in an excited scream and the need to faint.

"Hi, can I help you?" she asked after a moment.

My heart raced, "Yes, I'm here to pick up my husky, Wolf."

After a minute of clicking keys, her eyes glossed over and her expression went flat. Her eyebrows furrowed as she looked back up at me.

"He was already picked up," she said. My heart fell to the ground. My knees buckled together. My nose felt hot and the room grew small. I gripped the counter to keep from falling but its smooth texture was letting me go.

"Who picked him up?" I asked. Darkness flitted around the corners of my vision.

She pursed her lips, "It looks like it was the man who brought him in."

"Does he have a name?"

The girl grimaced, "I'm sorry, ma'am, I can't give out that information." I could see the fear in her eyes reflecting my own. I couldn't blame her even if I was tempted to yank her by the collar. She didn't know who I was. And I had no way to confirm it.

"Okay," I squeaked. I steadied my feet and stuffed the steel ball down in my chest. I hung my head as I drug myself out, not wanting to look at anyone in that room, certain they were all staring at me.

The air was sharp outside, biting my skin in a million tiny places. I strode into the small area of trees and grass beside the building in an attempt to escape. I tasted blood and only then realized I'd been biting my cheek to keep from crying. Swinging my head around, I scanned everywhere for Wolf. Someone had him. *Was it Marshall? It had to be. Was he using Wolf to bait me?* I held my breath and waited, hoping that was so. If not, someone else had him. A stranger. A stranger who saw him hurt and took him to the vet and is now gone.

I had nothing, no way of finding him. As the seconds passed without seeing Marshall or Wolf, the desire reared in me to storm back into that office. I remembered the pistol pulling at my waist. My hand hovered over my hip. Tears slipped down like a river in a wasteland. *That wasn't me.*

My knees hit the cold dirt and I buried my face into my lap. My head hurt from the grip of my fingers pulling out my hair. And for a moment, the physical pain evened out the tearing of my heart. The wind howled and spun an amber rainbow of leaves around me. I was caught in a kaleidoscope of suffering. My heart exploded with the agony of everything I've always held in and I screamed. I poured out all my pain, all the hurt. My past, my childhood, my innocence, my body, my home, my sanity - my - *best friend*.

No one noticed my scream over the screeching sound of a bus stopping in front of me. A flood of strangers, all stuck in their own heads, emptied to the sidewalk.

I glowered behind the low hanging branches. The irrational urge to punch the trunk of the pine in front of me sent me reeling back, stumbling down the slope and over a cement rectangle. I held my hands up, bracing for impact, but my balance caught up with my stupid fumbling legs.

The beanie on my head felt as far away as my sanity. I pulled it down, only so that I didn't lose what little I had left. I could care less about my appearance. The breeze swept through my sweater as if I were naked and I shivered.

Where was he? Why did this happen? A man in a white pollo gave me a raised eyebrow as he slid into his little shiny money on wheels. I grit my teeth while he pulled away. My feet carried me away from my madness...or perhaps it was the madness carrying me. It began only as a pace, back and forth, hoping. Holding on. Aching for the ice blue irises. But my life was destined to be gray. I looked up. I looked everywhere. No sky, no bird, no Wolf.

After what felt like forever, I walked away from the lot - defeated. The brown tops of my boots shuffled over the sidewalk cracks, my body functioning on its own with a mind that had gone numb. A headache cracked my skull and my lips tasted of salt. My chest heaved with shakes. When I looked up, I found myself in front of train tracks.

If my heart didn't feel so heavy, I might have laughed.

Maybe this was it. Where I was always supposed to end back up at. A voice called over a speaker, but I couldn't hear the words. An orange glow of lit up numbers and letters ran across a black electric screen, too blurred to see. I gripped onto my sleeves and stepped into a passenger car.

The seats were a washed out cobalt colored plastic and the floor was littered with memories of steps once taken. I grasped onto a black metal pole. The frigidness of it against my cheek was almost enough to shock me out of my stupor - but my heart hurt too much to care. Swishing movement sounded as more people entered.

With a shaky inhale, I shifted my gaze away from the dingy floor. Heat surged into my eyes when I saw the ad above the window. I gripped the pole so hard, a muscle twinged in my forearm. On the very end of it to the right was a little girl in pigtails sticking her tongue out to a man who imitated her, but his tongue stretched a foot in length to reach hers.

My mouth hung open with a scream I couldn't utter. My chest closed and tightened as if my entire body was constricting itself. I shook my head, trying to clear away what I was seeing.

"No," I whispered. Barely able to see through slitted eyes, I stamped forward. I reached for the ad but my fingers barely grazed the bottom of it.

"No. You can't do this!" I blurted. I climbed up on the seat, determination blocking out the shrinking room and blackened edges of my vision. My hand found the top of the paper, and I yanked it down with everything I had. The paper fell, torn like wings of a butterfly caught in a net.

A group of people stared at me. I held it up for them - let them see it. They should gawk at the lasciviousness of the image. They should be enraged. But they blinked back indifference.

"This is wrong!" I screamed and convulsed with unrelenting tears . They didn't react, didn't budge, didn't care. *How could they be like this?*

"Can't you see? They groom them. And they're desensitizing all of you. You don't see it. You NEVER SEE IT!" I shrieked and tore the crumpled paper to shreds.

"Hey, don't. Don't you think you're overreacting?" A man with spiky white curls held up his hand.

"Overreacting? Overreacting?! I bet you're one of them." I sneered and walked until I was inches from his thin face.

"I'll show you overreacting." I whispered, dropping the shreds, letting them flutter to the floor. In one swift motion, I reached into my side. The metal was no longer cold, it was the temperature of my womb, ready to birth. It pulled out with ease. My hand didn't shake as I leveled the barrel to his nose. I narrowed my eyes, all the muscles of my face pulling to the center. A tornado whirled through me. The man shrunk into the wall, edging up against the side of the hard seats.

"You men ruin souls, and you!" I screamed and turned the weapon towards the others.

"Stand by and *let it* fucking happen!" I swiveled back to the scared little man, barely able to see him past the tears in my eyes. A hand from behind me grasped my wrist and knocked the weapon into my side.

I blinked away the fog, "*You*," I whispered through clenched teeth. Marshall's brown eyes narrowed in on me. His hand became like steel around mine and his breath came in rapid short stutters as if he'd been running. I backed up until my spine hit the pole.

"Here to take me back?" I spat. His eyes flickered away and then came back to me, resolution settling over his face.

"Yes," he said.

I shook my head, rage boiling. I poured every ounce of hate through my eyes at him. He pulled his lips together with an inhale, causing his jaw to tighten. I slapped him and he staggered back, but he didn't loosen his grip. Why would he? That was the hand with the gun.

I raised the heel of my boot and smashed it down on his toes. A shock wave rolled up to my knee. A snarl emitted from my throat, I'd hit steel. His broad chest rose beneath his sweat damped shirt as he straightened, and his hand tightened even more around me. I tried to wrench myself out of his grip. My stomach churned as his touch spiraled through the veins in my arm like sharp electric stabs.

The train lurched forward, throwing me into his board of a body. The smell of smoke, pine, and sweat flooded my senses. With a grunt, I tried to push myself away, but he had my elbow now too. I looked at it over my left side, trying to make sense of the baby blue strap tethered around his wrist.

A second turned to an hour, paused by some force of confusion - disbelief. It was as if I was staring at the world through a magnifying glass and then it all collapsed into one pinpoint of light - and at the center…was Wolf.

My body went limp as he brushed against my calf. His face stared into me in patient expectation. I fell to him, and slipped from Marshall. Wolf made a low chuffle before nuzzling his jaw into my lap. I couldn't move. I couldn't do anything but blink.

I could hear Marshall saying my name, but it was at the end of an interminable tunnel. Wolf pawed at my thigh and I began to take in oxygen again. I wrapped my arms around his neck, enveloping my face into his fur. The familiar scent of earth and dog and his particular shampoo told me it was real. But my heart didn't want to let him go. I was afraid if I did, he might vaporize.

I could feel the presence of someone sitting next to me. Through the top of Wolf's white fur was Marshall. I couldn't read his face. I buried myself into Wolf again. It was almost too much. My head hurt. The familiar rattling of metal as Marshall emptied my pistol shook me from my stupor. I took a deep breath.

"You don't have to go," Marshall interrupted before I had a chance to say anything.

"What?" I squeaked. He looked at me head on as he put everything into the pocket of his brown leather jacket.

"I'm here to bring you back, but not by force." He lifted his hat and adjusted his feathery auburn hair as I stared in disbelief.

With a hand raised, he went on, "I'm not who you think I am, Jay. I'm not one of *them*," He lowered his voice to a guttural growl, "I'm the guy that hunts those bastards down."

I stared and clenched onto Wolf, "So why are you after me?" I whispered.

"Because, Jay, we need you"

"We?" My chest tightened.

He stood and held out his hand, but I scrunched my brows and climbed to my feet without his assistance. Wolf's body hugged my calf - a warm comfort in the cold train. The city flashed by in pieces of marble and stone. With tensed fists, I followed Marshall to a pair of empty seats, certain everyone was staring us down. But I refused to look.

He leaned forward on his thighs, "It's your parents."

My voice felt stuck.

"What about my parents?"

CHAPTER TWENTY-TWO

TRUST AND HATE

"What about my parents?!" I repeated as the train slowed to a screeching stop. Marshall stood, but didn't hold out his hand again. Instead, he shot a nod to the opening doors. With some reluctance, I followed him into the frostbitten air. He immediately shimmied out of his coat and handed it over when I started rubbing my arms.

I stared, unsure if I should accept.

"Are you going to take it or stand there and freeze?"

I snatched it, pulled out my gun and the ammo and handed it back. His lips drew into a straight line. I rolled my eyes and pretended not to be cold, yet bit the inside of my bottom lip to keep it from quivering.

"Come on, my car's a block down. We can take it somewhere and get you warmed up." Marshall began walking away.

"No," I stated. He turned around and I shook my head, the action causing the pendant at my collarbone to twirl.

"Are you nuts?"

"Maybe I am. But I'm done with people deciding what's best for me." I said. His eyes narrowed.

He sauntered forward, "And what is best for you?" he asked in a deep whisper, inches from touching me.

I shivered, but held my stance. "I'm not going anywhere until I know what's going on."

He hung his jaw. "Fine. About a month ago, my team busted the Cummings, your parents. They're awaiting trial. I was sent to find you. Your connection could help us locate and track down a very large and powerful trafficking circuit -"

"You expect me to believe this?!"

"You think I'm lying? That I'm what? Trying to trick you into coming with me?" His eyebrows were pinned down by what seemed like malice. But it didn't feel directed towards me. It was like I was looking into a reflection. My own pain and frustration laced the edges of his brows. Hate festered in the flecks of his irises.

I rubbed my forehead, "I don't know what to believe anymore."

His face softened, but the anger was still there, buried beneath jasper.

"You don't have to come," he sighed, "I won't force that on you."

I shifted and bit my lip. The last thing I wanted was to go back to Washington. No, that wasn't the last thing. My body not being my own was.

"If I go…and testify…would I…be safe from them finally?"

His eyes went wide and I swore I saw them tear up, but maybe I'd imagined it.

"If you come with me, I'll personally make sure of it. But I can't protect you if you stay." He wanted to protect me? He barely knew me. I barely knew him.

I thought for a moment, "Wouldn't I be in witness protection or something?"

"Probably."

"Probably? You don't know?" I wrapped my arms around my shoulders, it was getting colder every second I continued standing there, not to mention we were probably a long ways from his car after that train ride.

"I'm not in law enforcement. I don't know their procedures."

"So what are you?" I asked.

"A tracker."

I squinted, "Like..a bounty hunter?"

"Sort of," he shifted, "but I'm not after felons skipping bail. I go after the ones that haven't been caught."

I swallowed a breath. We held each other's eyes. I didn't know what he'd seen, or perhaps even what he'd been through. I didn't have to. The murky river of his eyes spoke every ounce of hatred I felt.

"What do I need to do?"

CHAPTER TWENTY-THREE

CONFESSIONS

When we turned the corner, and there was the little green Toyota, I froze. Marshall glanced at me, at the car, then back at me with a sheepish grin. I crossed my arms.

"Explain."

Marshall started with hands held up, "I didn't want to scare you off again."

"So you what, rented a car in two seconds before driving to the dog park?" I asked and then my expression went flat.

"Nah, borrowed."

"You mean you stole it."

"Borrowed, I gave it back."

"You *stole* a car."

"*Borrowed* a car."

"Stole," I raised my right eyebrow and tilted my head as he opened the passenger and side door.

"Borrowed." He yelled, jogging over to the driver's side.

I motioned Wolf to the back seat. He looked up at me before jumping in as if asking if it were okay. *Was it?* My heart stuttered for a moment. This could still be a trap.

Across the car, Marshall stared at me. Could it actually be

an ambush if he gave me my gun back? But it wasn't like it deterred him the first time. I rubbed Wolf's head as he sat on the cushion. I clenched my jaw and closed the door. I had to take a chance on freedom. I was tired of always looking over my shoulder. The engine cranked to life as I slipped in the front. I melted into the heat radiating from the dashboard. Ignoring the smirk in my peripheral, I rubbed my hands together and hovered them as close as possible to defrost the icicles they had become.

"You hungry?" he asked as he shifted into reverse.

I eyed him from behind my blonde curtain, "Starving."

We rode in silence with the only sound coming from the constant rattling of cheeseburger wrappers and the occasional soda slurp. I think we both felt overwhelmed with everything that had happened in the last few days. I grabbed my little square fry holder and leaned back into the seat. The wind howled, but it was distant behind the barrier of metal and glass. Specks of autumnal leaves littered the sky. I couldn't tell if there was snow mixed in or if it had ceased.

My mind wandered to my van, and the basket I'd left behind. I could've slapped myself for that but I'd already endured enough injuries for one week. I glanced at my jeans, amazed at the lack of bloodstain. Mayim did an incredible job washing them. I felt the eyes of Marshall on me as I had my shirt and sweater slightly lifted over the waistband. I patted my sweater back down and shifted in my seat as I heard the leathery crumple of a steering wheel.

I couldn't tell how long neither of us spoke, but the gray buildings disappeared, replaced by darkness dotted in sparkles of far off city lights. It was like being in a box with pinholes for air. I couldn't quite grasp why that was comforting.

"I'm sorry," Marshall said with an abruptness that shook me out of dozing off. When I turned to him, he was masked in shadows. Squares of light glided past his angled jaw as it poked out from behind his shoulder length hair. I held my lips, waiting for an explanation to the apology.

He cleared his throat, "I let that get out of hand. Neither of you should have been shot."

I sighed for a long time, "Why didn't you tell me who you were from the beginning?"

"Because," he said as his hands tightened around the wheel, "I didn't want to scare you off again and-"

"Again?"

"I obviously failed miserably," he muttered.

I kept silent and stared at the nothingness outside.

"*And* the longer I waited…the harder it got. The more nervous I became."

"Nervous? Why?" I scoffed. Like I could somehow be that intimidating.

Marshall sighed but he didn't answer my question. I pressed my forehead into the palm of my hand. He should have just left me alone. We were perfectly fine in Montana, Wolf and I. And I was getting better. At least I wanted to believe that. But if Marshall was able to find me, why couldn't the guy whose nose I broke? Or his employer? Did my escape cause his death? Is that why I lived without interruption for five years? Surely someone else could have been hired to drag me out of those mountains.

"You know what I don't get, now that I think about it," I started, "If you were the one after me this whole time, then who was the guy after me in the parking lot?"

Marshall sighed, "I don't know, do you still have his wallet?"

I grimaced, "No?"

"Could have been a retriever, could have been some random chump. No real way to know," Marshall said.

"Retriever? Makes it sound so innocent." I rolled my eyes as I imagined a golden furred puppy. Marshall mumbled under his breath.

"I still don't understand how I'm supposed to do anything," I said.

"What do you mean?" he asked.

"How is my testimony going to stop anyone from coming after me? I was safe. I was hidden. I was perfectly fine before *you* showed up,"

"One," he grinned, "You were not and still are not fine. And two, it wasn't that hard to find you so I highly doubt you were exactly safe."

He paused and nodded towards my feet, "You never did mention how you got that nasty cut at your ankle either, so without anyone's help you're already an endangerment to yourself."

"Who are you?" I gawked.

"Nobody," he said.

I huffed, "Even if it wasn't a rhetorical question, that's a stupid answer."

"Who I am is just not that important," he shrugged. I rolled my eyes even though it was too dark for him to see.

"You know, *apparently*, way more about me, than I do about you. Which is hardly fair considering."

"Considering what?"

My heart jumped at his agitation, "Considering I'm kinda at

your mercy right now."

His body slumped back into the seat "What do you want to know?" There was a lot I wanted to know. Like, how he found me - so easily at that. But there was a more important question.

"You really think I can help stop them?" I asked almost too quietly to hear. I studied the lines of his face, a gray outline against the night. His jaw flexed, but the rest of his muscles were stone.

"I think you're the best chance we have."

"How?" It's not like I had that much of a connection.

"I know it's not much to go on, but if you can identify who your parents sold you to, we'd be a lot closer than we ever have."

"But I never actually saw who I was sold to…just the middle man. I mean…that's who I always assumed he was," I crossed my arms, "Wouldn't my parents be a better witness to all of that?"

He nodded, "If they would speak. They're refusing. It was a miracle they got riled up enough to slip up about their block headed teen."

"I am not a-"

"Their words, not mine"

I smiled grimly, "Oh."

"Tell me something," his voice was low, matching the deep hum of the engine, "how did you escape?"

I fiddled with the rim of my beanie, "Honestly, I'm not even sure."

His head swung violently my way, "What?"

"Technically," I eyed him from the corner of my vision, "I busted his nose and ran onto a train before the doors closed."

"And the not so technical part?"

"The timing…was too perfect." I said.

"Maybe. Sometimes things happen that way."

"Yeah but…" I wanted to tell him about the blue jay but fear swirled in the corners of my heart. It was a silly thing to think a blue jay saved me. It had to be a coincidence, right? My gut screamed that it was a lie. There *was* something to that bird.

"Never mind," I whispered. How could he understand when I couldn't even grasp it myself? The dimness of the car grew lighter as we neared another city. I pulled my sleeves down and tucked my knees into my chest as if to crawl into a shadow and wished more than anything that we were in my van instead.

"When do you think we can get my van back?" I asked.

He hung his mouth open, "I don't know."

I scratched my forehead under the brim of my beanie, "Well that sucks…my home is now stuck in a compound until who knows when … and all my information was stolen."

"Wanna repeat that last bit?" he asked in an octave too high for someone so big. I winced as I recollected leaving out the part about being robbed when I told him about my van. We couldn't get it then because of a time restraint. So I said okay and kept silent.

"Yeah, I might have been robbed too." I shrugged.

"Fuck!" he burst out. I reeled into the side of the door. My eyes widened as he slammed a fist into the dashboard. He flexed his hand and shook it.

"Sorry," Marshall muttered as I clutched the door handle.

"What was that?" I squeaked.

He sighed as he rubbed his knuckles, "I'm just really doing a piss poor job is all."

"It's not your fault," I said.

He shot me a sideways glance, "Except it is."

"I think you had more important things to think about than locking up my van."

"It should have never come to that."

"Well, it did," I said, and crossed my arms, "and you can't change that. Just like…"

"What?" he asked when I trailed off and let the silence swallow us for far too long.

"Nothing, forget it." I said. The last thing I wanted to do was bring up my past. He probably knew enough to speculate. I couldn't possibly admit to it all. Not to anyone. But especially not to him. Judging by his anger every time the traffickers were brought up, his standards were about as high as mine. And I wasn't sure yet if that was endearing or terrifying. And as I contemplated a man whose face filled with rage at the mention of sexual abuse, I wondered why. He called them monsters. He hunts them down. Was he the reason my parents were in jail? It didn't take long for my thoughts to lull me to sleep. For the first time in a long time, I felt safe.

"Jay…" a voice beckoned me awake. I blinked to a bright glare lighting up the dark. Red lights blared in front of me. Brakes.

"Are we there?" the question rolled out of my mouth.

"A pit stop," he said. I squeezed my eyes shut and then open as we pulled into a lit parking lot. A yellow glow illuminated the building.

"I can sleep in a car." I reminded him, suddenly feeling my heart race at the thought of sharing a room.

"So can I," he said as he unclicked his seat belt with his battered fingers.

"Then what are we doing here?"

"Well," he said, "what I can't do is shower in a car."

"So? It's not like you stink." *Was I pleading now?*

He smiled, "Thanks, Jay. Nevertheless it's been a week. I'd feel better with a shower and we could both use a bed," he stated. I swallowed, though I knew he didn't mean the same bed.

"Do they even take dogs?" I tried. He raised an eyebrow and opened the door.

Standing, he looked down at me, "You don't really think I'd even consider a hotel that wouldn't allow him, do you?" and I swear I melted right out of that car.

CHAPTER TWENTY-FOUR

ONE BED

My head and stomach swirled when I walked in the room. I'd been outside with Wolf while Marshall paid. Needless to say, I had no idea what to expect. "I guess this is what happens when you book a room at one in the morning," I chuckled. A heavy sighing grunt came from Marshall as he whisked past me into the bathroom. Wolf limped to the right side of the only bed in the room, circled twice and then plopped to the floor.

I also plopped, but onto the mahogany comforter that smelled of dust and questions. My eyes shot to the bathroom door swinging open. I didn't even realize I'd dozed off…again. I sat up as Marshall walked out, his hair wet and slicked back. No baseball cap. Our eyes met and I looked away. A sweet shampoo haze brushed my face as I ran into the bathroom.

I stood in front of the mirror, debating whether or not to take a shower too. But then I remembered I didn't have a change of clothes. A knock sounded at the door and I shook in surprise.

I cleared my throat, "Yeah?"

"You don't have a change of clothes do you?" he asked with a hollow voice.

"Um, no." Could he read my mind?

"Of course you don't. You can borrow a shirt and we can get you something when we get to Spokane."

I bit my lip, "Okay…"

"I have the shirt here if you want it," he said. I opened the door, causing my hair to whip back. The shirt was clenched in his fists, but his eyes didn't meet mine. I finally grabbed it when he put his hand forward. I shut the door until only a slit was left.

"Marshall?"

"Yeah?"

"Thank you," I said. His chest expanded and his chin raised. His eyes met mine through the slit and then he nodded and walked away. I closed the door and stared down at his black shirt. It looked so much bigger in my hands.

When I slipped the shirt over my damp hair, it fell down to my mid thigh. How did his body make this look so small? I pulled it up and winced as my wrist grazed the purpled part of my side. I was thankful I didn't have to change the bandaging anymore. It was shocking how fast it had healed. I tried to tie the bottom of the shirt into a knot, but the knob bit looked ridiculously large. So I pulled my jeans on and let the top hang like a nightgown.

The girl staring back at me in the mirror felt like a stranger. A silver glimmer around my neck caught my eye. I pulled the necklace out from under the long black shirt. Maybe I should've looked harder for blue before, and realized I'd been carrying it all along.

I opened the door to find Marshall asleep on the floor, facing away from me. Wolf, curled up beside him, raised his head. I crawled into the bed and plopped into the pillow.

"Traitor," I whispered. He sighed and nuzzled his nose back into his paws. I rolled over and stared at the ceiling. My body felt as if it were on a ride, spinning and swirling and yet the world was still. After everything, it felt odd to be at rest. I didn't know what I was going to face tomorrow. And I knew my heart wasn't ready. My parents' faces, the way they looked, ignoring me as I screamed, flashed in my mind and I had to clutch at my chest. I squeezed my eyes shut as if that would erase the memory.

Marshall had far too much confidence in me. But why? I glanced over at his back. Was he really asleep or was his mind as violently awake as mine? His shirt was soft in my hand. I lifted it up to my nose, remembering that's what he smelled like up close. *What am I doing?*

"What are you doing?" Marshall asked. I dropped the neck of his shirt. He was staring at me. *When did he turn my way?!*

"Nothing." I squeaked.

"Uh huh," he said in a distant sleep bogged voice. I'm certain that if the lights were on, he could've seen the red in my cheeks.

"Goodnight," I said and turned to face the wall. He didn't answer back. Maybe he wouldn't remember in the morning.

Something heavy was on me. The weight compressed my chest into my lungs. A small shift and I could grasp at air again. My hands sifted through Wolf's soft fur. And then I bolted up.

"What are you doing up here?" I asked the animal as if he might respond. I glanced at his leg, still wrapped in bandages, but he seemed perfectly okay. His nose poked my cheek and then he licked my face. As I lay back down, I heard Marshall shuffle on the floor. *Did he put Wolf up here with me?*

Before I had time to give it more thought, I was out again, swallowed in the comfort of Wolf beside me, his head nestled under my chin.

The next time I woke up, Marshall was standing over me with a steaming cup in his right hand and a brown paper bag in the left. I shifted to my elbows.

"Morning," he said with a grin. I grimaced.

"What's that?" I nodded to the bag. He raised it up and took an over- exaggerated whiff.

"Breakfast."

I raised an eyebrow, "Okay, nobody is this nice."

He pursed his lips, "I did shoot you. And your dog"

"True," I snatched the bag from his hand. Inside were greasy hash brown squares and breakfast burgers. My stomach growled. I took one of each out and handed the bag back. He replaced my empty hand with the coffee.

I sighed, "As much as I'm enjoying all this, you don't have to keep making up for what happened. In fact, I'd rather you not." I took a crunch of the hashbrown, "Just be you, as terrible or as..well whatever you are. Just please don't be someone you're not."

He sat on the bed beside me, causing me to unintentionally lean in his direction.

"This is me," he stated, "and I'll keep making it up to you until you know that."

I swallowed. I stared at his lips for far too long and then swung my head away.

"Whatever," I mumbled and sipped the coffee, hiding the wince from the singe to my tongue. Beyond the partially opened wine colored curtains, an orange morning light bounced off two yellow arches. Marshall pulled them open more to light up the room. I was thankful for a cloudless sky. But going back to Washington meant it wouldn't be like that forever. Maybe when all this was said and done, I'd move somewhere dry and warm. Like Nevada or Arizona.

Marshall clapped his hands together with a wry look on his face, "Ready?"

I coughed, "No."

He genuinely looked worried. I rolled my eyes and hustled across the navy carpet to the bathroom.

"I'm never going to be ready, not really," I stated and shut the door.

"Jay," he called from the other side.

"Yup?" I asked with my pants pulled down, wondering if I'll

ever have a private moment again.

"It's going to be okay," he said, his voice partially muffled by the door.

I scoffed, "You don't know that. You don't know that at all."

"Jay..." he said as I ran my hands under the water. What was he doing? Why was he doing it? He needed to stop. I swung open the door to see him leaning against the wall, damn bulging chest straining through his tight white shirt underneath his leather jacket.

"I'm going to make sure it will be," his voice was low, honeysuckle eyes burning into me.

"Do what you want," I spat, "but for the love of God, up your shirt size." I brushed past, electricity firing up my entire left side from grazing him. I grabbed Wolf's leash and headed out while Marshall stood, silent, mouth open at me.

Every emotion wanted to boil out of me, but I stuffed it down. I didn't want him to see me lose it again and I needed to get out of that room before I did something I regretted. I was not about to be fooled into someone's bed. It would be on my terms, on my time, with the right person. Which I didn't even believe existed. But Marshall was doing a damn good job of trying to convince me otherwise.

But was this nice guy stuff all an act? History told me yes, no matter how much I wanted to believe the fantasy and fall into his strong arms. My heart ached from how much it meant that he cared about me. But I, under no circumstances, could fall for it. And so after a potty walk with Wolf, when I found Marshall waiting by the passenger side door to open it, I wanted nothing more than to punch him in the face. My expression must have told him, because he instantly looked dejected. And a part of me felt bad. Because what if...

…it wasn't an act?

CHAPTER TWENTY-FIVE

ALONE IN HIS APARTMENT

I traced my finger along the edge of the cool window. We didn't talk other than what was necessary. It was almost 3pm when we passed the sign welcoming us to Spokane. I never asked what town our final stop was in, but this was where he'd said we'd pick me up some clothes. My childhood home was only an hour away from here. The ticking of my heart thudded enough to make me queasy.

A brick building the shade of a cardinal caught my attention. There were trees like claws scaling its sides. It was devastatingly beautiful with one of its windows punctured by an intrusive branch. I pulled my sleeves over my knuckles seeing the Spokane river and remembering the fifth grade field trip to the Museum of Arts and Culture. Back when I had friends and us girls huddled in the seat together, giggling about our favorite songs, the cutest boys, and the dreams we had. We were inspired by the field trip and later that week I began my journey in painting. It lasted less than a week before being crushed.

Pulling into a shopping plaza, I wondered for the first time if that temporary dream was destroyed out of my parents' fear. In fact, any time I considered any kind of career it seemed to have been trampled, ridiculed, or shunned. How did I not see that?

I was still lost in my mind when Marshall turned the engine off.

"You good?" he asked, his voice a damper to my troubling thoughts. I nodded with a smile and a light sparkled in his eyes. Hope. What he was hoping for, I wasn't sure. But I liked his smile and I was tired of the silence, but my heart was scared.

"I'll just walk Wolf real quick," I said before I went in to find some clothes.

"Come on, bud." I said opening the door. He was stretched out on the entire length of the back seats. He yawned and popped his head up but didn't budge.

"Come on," I insisted with a light voice. Marshall whistled and Wolf jumped out. I shot him a quizzical look. He only shrugged in return.

"You know, he did that to you," I said to Wolf, pointing at his bandaged leg. Wolf didn't care. He was far too busy with his nose shoved into the ground, hunting for the perfect spot. All while Marshall leaned against the passenger side of the car and watched us with his eyes hidden under the shadow of his ball cap.

What would he do if we took off? Probably run after us. I doubt we'd get far. Each of us with a slight limp. And as my heart fluttered, I wondered if running was something I really wanted to do. Not to mention, I wouldn't only be running away from Marshall…I'd be running out on every girl that needed my help. A tornado whirled in me. If I could stop others from being hurt and used like we were nothing more than toys, then I was going to fight with everything I had. No matter how much that scared me. I may not be convinced there was any good left in this poisoned world, but I could combat that by doing good - even if no one else would.

"Did you get everything you need?" Marshall asked as I slid into the front seat with an enormous plastic bag in my hands.

"Yes, for the hundredth time," I rolled my eyes. Wolf popped up and pressed his cold wet nose against my cheek, eliciting a squeak from me. Marshall jumped before side-eyeing me as I burst into laughter.

"Jumpy, are we?" I asked as his hand wrapped around the back of my head. The lighthearted feelings that had swept me up a moment ago were swallowed into another galaxy. My body deflated as his hand found my headrest, not me.

He smirked at me before staring out the back window to pull out of the parking spot. The way he concentrated, eyes pulled into focus, every muscle fiber taught, made my breath come out like opening an oven and my insides all mush. His leather jacket crinkled as he slipped his arm back to the gear shift between us.

I bit my lip and pulled away to gaze out my window. *What the hell is wrong with me? Get it together Jay, don't fall for him.* But the thing with falling is, no one ever intends to. It just happens, whether by accident - or carelessness. And at the end of a fall, is always pain.

"What are you thinking about?" Marshall asked after ten minutes of silence.

"Uh," I stuttered, "Nothing really, just staring at the clouds." Which was true. I was watching them feather out in the wind, weaving and bobbing as bits of sky jutted out like the lines of a puzzle.

"Mmm," he mumbled.

"What about you?" I turned to face him.

"Nothing really, just staring at the road." He matched my statement. I rolled my eyes.

"Don't tell me you're as boring as I am," I said.

He scoffed, "Nothing wrong with boring, but *you* are *far* from it."

"Oh? And what about me do you find *so fascinating*?" I exaggerated my tone.

"Everything."

I gripped the plastic in my hands and narrowed my eyes at him, "ehhh, cop out."

"You want specifics?" He shifted in his seat, "You observe every detail, but you aren't looking for flaws, you're hoping something good will surprise you. Or how you hide beneath your layers, all the while wishing someone would see you - really see you."

I twirled my new necklace, "And you think you see me, Marshall?"

"More than you know, less than I'd like."

"What does that me-" I started as we pulled into an apartment complex. Wolf popped up, recognizing the slowing of the vehicle.

With a bag of clothes clutched in my arms, I stared at an old terra cotta apartment behind the windshield. The windows were single paned and one of them on the second story was open with a small sheer curtain waving to us.

"Shit," Marshall muttered, straining up at the building.

"What?" I asked.

"Oh nothing, I just left my window open all week." He grumbled. My eyes widened and I squeezed my bag.

"This," my eyes darted to the looming architecture, "is your place?"

"Yes, ma'am."

I pulled at my beanie, "I thought we were going to speak with a...actually, I don't know who we were going to speak to."

"A lawyer, but our appointment isn't until tomorrow." He said and clicked out of his seatbelt.

"I...think I'll just...stay here." I said. I'd never been to a man's place. Not without it being about sex. Without warning, all those memories started overwhelming my senses. My body was recognizing the danger long before the logical part of my brain could reason with it. My face felt hot, my heart vibrating faster than a hummingbird and the corners of my vision blurred. I swear I could even smell the sickening scent of cinnamon.

"If that's what you want," Marshall's cavernous voice disrupted the dissociation from progressing. I blinked at him as I felt Wolf's fur on my shoulder. I leaned my head in the softness.

"I don't want you to feel uncomfortable, Jay," Marshall said, "but, if I was going to do something, I'd have done it a long time ago." I swiveled my head back at him.

"It's never too late to change your mind," I said, narrowing my eyes.

He sighed, "I suppose you're right. My apartment is 17 on the second floor…if you change your mind." And he left. I sat in the seat, feeling along the bottom for a handle. My back ached as I pushed into a lying position. I was alone finally. The evening sun broke through the window, highlighting the dust and fragments of fiber in the air. I stretched my hand to the light, weaving my fingers through the beams.

The abrupt opening of the car door startled me into an upright position as I grappled for my gun. It was only Marshall, with a giant white comforter in his hands.

"I thought you might get cold," he said and threw it over me. I glanced down at it then up at him.

"Thanks…" I said. He nodded and shut the door. He still had his leather jacket on as he walked back up the soot colored staircase and my face flushed with heat as I observed the large V of his back. Our eyes briefly met as his hand went for the door. I sucked in my breath. He tipped his head as a welcome gesture, but I shook an emphatic no. I almost laughed when he slumped like a pouting toddler and went in only to return a second later with a crooked grin and a thumbs up. I imitated his hand sign. I was good. Perfectly good out here. Then he went back in for the final time and I almost felt empty.

I never had a boyfriend before. It wasn't allowed. I wasn't allowed to feel or fall in love. Though, like most young girls, I desperately wanted to. Sitting there in the passenger side of the car made it easy to slip back into the memory of my mothers reprimand.

We spent the morning at the mall. And I met a boy. He was cute with side swept bangs and a crooked smile. I knew him from school, but he'd never spoken to me before now. Butterflies fluttered all through me as we exchanged numbers.

But mom was never too far out of sight.

Back in the car as I sipped on a coke, my thoughts were wrapped around the boy and forgot all about the client I had to see at three. Out of the silence, my mother asked for my phone. I didn't think anything of it, but nearly choked when she threw it out the window.

"You can never have a boyfriend," she scolded, "Do you understand?!" then she cleared her throat and continued in a softer voice, "You're not girlfriend material. You're too used. No one wants someone like you for a girlfriend. It's just - not who you are." My head felt heavy. I wanted to scream at her *And whose fault is that?!* But I held my tongue and clutched at the hold in the door, unable to take another sip of my drink.

I blinked back the memory and leaned in the seat, curling up beneath the massive marshmallow cloud. It didn't smell like anything, unlike the t-shirt I was wearing. It wasn't long before my eyes felt as heavy as lead. Panic dashed into my veins and I shot up again. The doors still weren't locked. I dove for the locking mechanism on the driver's side. A twinge went through my back as I leaned for it.

The numbness in my hips made me decide against locking the door just yet. So I opened it and hopped out. I bent over and reached for the ground, feeling the familiar pull in the back of my legs, easing out the hours of tension that had built in there. I leaned to my side and breathed through the stretch in my hips. I stood and twisted, popping my spine in about twenty places.

When I opened the car door again, nothing in me wanted to go back and lay in that uncomfortable seat. I sighed and glanced at the open window. It still wasn't shut. A tingle prickled along my arms and down my neck. I strained to see into the room, curious if he was in there, watching. Did he know that I might be contemplating going up?

I whined and grabbed the comforter, feeling a pang in my gut. I was pretty sure it was hunger and not dread this time. Wolf, without hesitation, leaped out, his nails clicking against the floorboard.

I took a hold of the leash and made my way up the stairs. My boots echoed through the air. Yeah, Marshall had to know I was coming. It felt a little like defeat. But I hadn't given in to anything yet. I could always say no. And Wolf would back me up, even if he had taken a liking to Marshall. I glanced down at him by my side.

"Wouldn't you buddy?" I asked but he didn't respond. We continued the climb. I kept expecting to see the door open, but even as I reached it, it remained closed. I didn't know if I should knock or try the handle. I didn't want to be invasive. It felt rude not to knock.

So I wrapped my knuckles on it a few times, shaking the metal seven with each blow. But there was no answer. I waited another minute and raised my fist to the door again but it opened before I could touch it. Marshalls' face poked out of the crack, his hair dripping over his face.

"Nice timing," he smiled and as I saw a glistening bare shoulder, I realized I had caught him in the middle of a shower.

"I'll wait out here…until you're done." I said, quickly turning away. The door closed behind me and I gulped for air. My head was spinning, but in a good way this time. I steadied the shaking of my hands. I let my eyelids fall and breathed in through my nose…slow…steady. The breeze whistled in my ear, rolling over my body in waves of soundless echoes. I let the air out of my lungs and turned back to the door, just in time for it to open again.

Marshall waved me in, bowing with a smile as I entered. I rolled my eyes at him. But I couldn't help the smile that crept onto my face when I noticed the looseness of his shirt. I felt a bit taken aback as I stared at an empty living room with one white mattress in the center of the floor. In the far corner near the open window was a black velvet chair.

There was no table, no tv, no books, pictures, nothing cluttering the counters. In the distance I could hear a rumble and drip. The smell of coffee told me what that sound was. Realizing I was still wearing the comforter like a cape, I thrust it onto the bed and wiped my hair from my face.

"Do you not come here often?" I gave a nervous laugh.

"Mmm...no..." he said flatly and locked the door. Did I just make the biggest mistake of my life? I eyed him as he strode to the kitchen.

"Coffee?" he asked

"Uhhh. Not really..." I said, glancing out the window at the bright orange of a setting sun.

"Of course...beer?" he asked, pulling open the fridge with a strained look on his face.

"Not really getting any better." I laughed and scratched my forehead under my beanie.

"Right," he said and closed the door, hands on his hips. His eyes searched the floor for some kind of answer. Then he grabbed his phone off the counter and walked to a back room.

Wolf jumped up on the pristine white bed, smudging it with his paws. A short hollow scream tumbled out of my lips as I pushed Wolf off and began patting away the marks. I just about had it gone when Marshall came back in the room.

"I hope you like Asian."

"Food?" I asked.

"Uh...yeah..?"

I sat on the edge of the bed, "You're not used to guests are you?"

"Is it that obvious?"

I pursed my lips, "I would know"

"Yes, very much out of practice." He laughed and gathered his hair into a cinnamon roll size bun.

"Well...what happened," I asked, "you know my dark past, but I don't know anything about yours."

"What makes you think I have a dark past?" he asked.

"Do you?"

He folded his arms, covered in long black sleeves, and leaned against the counter. I bit my lip in anticipation.

"Yes...and no. Not like yours...exactly."

"Exactly? What does that mean?"

He blew out a puff of air, "I had a good upbringing, but I've seen a lot with this job."

My eyes cast to the floor, thinking instantly of what he might've seen. Or what he might know about what goes on behind closed doors. What kind of evil had he been exposed to and how did that make him feel about me? He knew things that I never told anyone, things I kept locked up. Things I couldn't bring myself to admit, even if they weren't my fault.

What were his secrets? We all have things we don't want the world to know. Little skeletons that become invisible suitcases we lug around. When I looked back up at Marshall, his eyes were glazed over, lost in a memory. He shook his head and smiled at me as if nothing had happened.

"So why the empty apartment?" I asked, changing the subject.

He pulled the corner of his cheeks tight.

"Did you just move in?"

He laughed low, and to himself, "Been here three years now." He said wiping a dry forehead.

My eyes went wide, "Okay...explain."

He opened his mouth but a knock at the door turned both of our attention. He held his hand up and peeked out the peephole. I knew they called it fast food, but that seemed a little too fast.

CHAPTER TWENTY-SIX

HAUNTED TOUCH

Turns out, the pho restaurant was only across the street. I followed Marshall and the sweet aroma into the kitchen where he started emptying out squares of styrofoam on the counter.

He handed me a fork as I picked up a bowl of thinly sliced veggies and noodles covered in salty gold liquid. Before I could begin eating, my stomach sang in monster notes of appetite. As if I wasn't about to satisfy it.

"So, you were saying?" I asked between blows to the hot food.

He looked at me while shoveling a forkful. I waited for him to swallow. Dude was hungry. Why did we wait so long to get food?

"Well, I suppose it's simple. As a tracker…I'm just not here much." I nodded. It made sense I guess. Until I realized it was missing something.

"But there's like nothing here at all. Not even boxes."

He tipped his fork to me, "You haven't seen every room."

I shrugged my shoulders and slurped down more noodles, "Fair enough."

He chucked his plate into the trash as I let Wolf finish off mine. I wiped my face with a napkin and strode to the fridge. He stared at me as I pulled out two beers. He raised an eyebrow.

"I changed my mind…about the beer."

"You sure?" he asked, his hand hovering over the one I held out to him.

"It's not like you can get drunk off of just one." I shrugged.

"Besides," I admitted, "I think we could both relax just a bit." My worried, frantic mind needed to rest and I wasn't all too ready to talk to a lawyer or see my parents or admit to their crimes. Or somehow identify the man that tried to drag me away to who knows where five years ago. What was it Marshall said? My parents were connected to a large and powerful trafficking circuit. I shuddered at what that might've meant for me if I hadn't escaped.

Marshall furrowed his eyebrows and his eyes darkened. With a long sigh, he grabbed both beers. His fingers grazed mine, causing me to bite my lip to keep from yanking back. He didn't seem to notice. With a pop and fizzle, the cap released. I took the cold glass bottle back, careful not to touch his fingers this time, though the fire welling deep inside me desired nothing more. I wanted to be touched, to be held, to be loved. And a part of me hated that I wanted it so bad, terrified at the thought. And yet with each sip of alcohol, my desire to throw caution to the wind and say *screw it* grew.

"You know," Marshall said, leaning an elbow on the counter, slowly sipping at the amber bottle, "You're incredibly strong."

"What do you mean?" my question echoed into my bottle as I took a giant swig.

"With everything you've been through, you keep pushing back. Against it all, you never stop fighting," he said. I rubbed my eyes, and peered at my more than half empty beer. My vision moved slower than normal. *Was I really already affected? I couldn't be, right?* My stomach twisted in a knot. *What was I doing?*

"What exactly is it I've been through?" I asked, walking over to the counter opposite him, putting us at barely more than arms reach. I was curious about how much he knew. He stared at me as his knuckles whitened around the practically full liquor.

He twisted the bottle in his hand and seemed to look through me instead of at me, "You were trafficked from the time you were six until the time you were eighteen when your parents sold you to the black market, but you escaped, causing them to lose the money they received unless-"

I felt as if my body was going to slide out from under me. The slick beer in my hand slipped from my grasp and Marshall, faster than I thought could be possible, was there catching it, ready to catch me. The worried glaze of his eyes made me wonder if I looked like I might pass out.

"How do you know that?" I whispered.

"Your parents admitted to it in questioning."

"You questioned them?"

"No," he shook his head, "the detective on our team did." I nodded, not fully understanding how his team operated.

I put my face in my hands, *"I was six?"* the question rolled off in a faint smoke. It wasn't meant to be answered but I could feel the stiffening of Marshall beside me. I knew I was young, but I couldn't remember how young. I wasn't even sure if my first memory was...my first. The tears collected like a puddle in my eyes and my chest felt heavy. *Why? Why did this have to happen to me? Why couldn't I have a normal life?*

I took a shaky breath and looked up at Marshall, "Oh, I'm

real strong," I said, my voice thick with sarcasm. His face scrunched up in a mixture of sadness and anger.

"Someone lied to you," he breathed, "when they made you believe your tears were a sign of weakness." His finger glided along my cheek, feeling like a feather and the tip of a lit sparkler all at once. I turned my cheek into the palm of his hand, surprising us both.

As I straightened, his hand slid down to my shoulder, sending chills throughout my body in uncontrollable waves. We were breathing slow, deep, in unison. I stared into honey under the veil of dark lashes. His hand gently squeezed my shoulder as my eyes fell to his soft lips.

"Jay," he whispered, his breath warm on my face as I inched closer. Our foreheads met and I closed into darkness. Every part of me tingled. My chest heaved and a familiar smell swirled around me in a haze. *Him.* He didn't move, didn't press in, his fingers still wrapped around my shoulder. I flicked my lashes open to eyes that spoke things I wish his mouth would utter.

Our lips grazed and a movie reel flicked on before me. My gut turned and without warning I curled away, peeling his fingers from me. It was an uncontrollable thing, as if my body acted on its own. My chest closed in and I turned my face from Marshall. I couldn't see what I'd done to him.

The sound of glass shattering made me whip back around. There was beer and blood all over the counter, flowing over the edge and pooling onto the ground. I stared in disbelief at the shattered bottle. Marshall's jaw clenched shut as, he too, stared - perplexed at the mess. I reached out to help, but he held up his other hand.

I wanted to crawl inside myself. Marshall looked to the

ceiling, holding in his breath. He turned to the sink and flicked on the water. I clasped my arms over my chest and flitted with the edge of my sweater, unsure of what to do. Behind me was a barrier of cabinets. In front of me was a man that just crushed a beer bottle with his bare hand when I didn't kiss him.

I pressed my nails into my forearm, hoping the pain would keep in the tears. Marshall didn't say a word. I peeked around the corner, suddenly wondering where Wolf was. Did the noise startle him? I couldn't see him from where I was, but he hadn't trotted over to investigate either.

Marshall peered up at me as he leaned over the sink. His eyes darted back to the running water. He flicked it off and strode down the hall with an explicative. My heart raced. I should have stayed in the car. *Dumbass.* I walked over the mess on the floor, grabbed my bag of clothes and reached for the door with Wolf on my tail, sensing the panic rising in me.

I had it open an inch before a hand slammed it shut. I stared at Marshall, his eyes red and wide. I stepped back, binding up the bag in my fist.

"Before you go, please, give me two seconds." He pleaded. I didn't want to give him anything. But I wasn't sure I had that choice.

"Fuck." He whispered, looking away and holding in his bottom lip. The same lip I'd been touching moments before. I sniffled and cast my gaze to the ground. I didn't want to look at him. Not after an outburst like that.

"Let me go," I whispered. I didn't need an explanation. Men couldn't handle not getting what they wanted.

"Jay, please." He moved closer, but didn't grab for me, though I could see his fingers almost reach out.

I met his eyes, "No." I pushed past him and yanked the door

open.

"I couldn't save her," he said as I whipped outside.

I turned back, "What?"

He wasn't looking at me. His hands were balled into fists and his chest shook as he uttered his next bewildering statement.

"My sister was just like you."

CHAPTER TWENTY-SEVEN

THE AIR BETWEEN US

"What are you talking about?" I asked, twisting my fingers through the plastic handles as Wolf switched his gaze between us. Marshall hadn't moved, hadn't looked up from the spot on the ground he was staring at. The evening wind wavered between us as if trying to force us together. But I refused to go back in there.

"I'm sorry. You reminded me of her."

I pulled my hair out of my face, "I reminded you of your sister?!"

His mouth hung open, "Oh god, no, not then…after."

"Marshall," I shook my head and leaned to my non-injured hip, "what the hell are you talking about?"

He wiped half his face, making a crackling sound over his scruff.

"She was fifteen and depressed, before she ran away. It was worse when she came back. She didn't like to be touched. Like you. In the end though, she couldn't hang on and I wasn't there."

"She…?" I didn't want to finish the sentence. I didn't know if I could if I tried. The words were stuck in my throat. I felt like I'd been run over by a semi with that statement. Marshall nodded and now I understood why his face was blotchy. I understood why he broke that bottle. It wasn't because of what I didn't do. Marshall wasn't some client I was forced to kiss.

A tree stood in the middle of the complex with half of its branches naked and half decked in spots of orange. Like me, it was barely hanging on. I'd spent so many days over the past five years not knowing if I could continue. Physically I'd escaped, but mentally, I was still back there. And as much as I hated them, my parents and the varying abusers, I hated myself more. I hated that I was silent. I hated that I didn't fight. I hated how weak I was. And every time I lost control of my senses, my body, and my thoughts - I was reminded of that weakness. Had it not been for Wolf and the idea of him being alone, I might've allowed a climbing accident to happen to me. I would have let go. I would have finally been free.

"I understand if you don't want to stay the rest of the night. I'm sorry." Marshall said across the breeze. It took two seconds for me to bridge the gap and cross back over his threshold. He moved out of my way, though part of me didn't want him to. But I fought the urge to repeat what I had just caused. Even if I'd misread the entire situation.

Wolf, with his head tipped to the side, waited on the balcony. I tugged at his leash with a nod and he trotted back in - all the way to the bed. He knew better than I had apparently. Somehow he sensed something good about Marshall.

"So you're not mad at me?" I asked. I had to be sure, but maybe I shouldn't have waited until I was back inside before I asked.

He shook his head, "Never."

Cold air howled into the room. Marshall stood by the open

door, his hand gripping the golden handle with his eyes locked onto me. I attempted to ignore the cocktail of emotions surging through my body. My head felt light and my arms tingled.

"Well," I said and settled onto the mattress, "If you don't hate me, I'll stay."

He closed the door and dropped his head, "How could I hate you?"

"Because..." I bit my lip and cast my eyes to the ground, "of how I reacted." I didn't know how to say all that I wanted. I didn't know how to apologize for his sister or for letting my bizarre emotions take control. I didn't know how to tell him how much I wanted to wrap myself into him and was yet repulsed when I got close. I didn't even know if he felt the same about me. Maybe all his kindness, all his chivalry, was never about *me.* The image of his stiffness sparked in my mind. A big part of me wasn't sure if my repulsion was because of the memories or the intimacy and I was terrified that if I tried again, it would flood in and sweep me away completely.

"Jay..." he whispered my name in a way that made my heart flicker, "I'm an idiot."

I scoffed and rubbed my arm where the imprints of his grip were a fading memory. The subtle swish of his feet along the faux wood floor stopped in front of me.

"Why?" I asked, "Because you flipped out? Because, I- I caused that." My voice came up an octave, still very aware I hadn't said anything about his sister. The one that I reminded him of. Was he afraid I would take my life? Is that why he was so adamant in his praises? Did he really think any of those words he said? Or were they the unsaid thoughts he wished he could have said to her?

"You didn't know what you were doing," he said.

I grit my teeth, "I knew exactly what I was doing."

"Then tell me," he said, still standing over me like a looming tower, "Was I the first guy since you escaped?"

"What does that have to do with anything?"

He sighed and walked to the chair in the corner of the room after closing the window next to it. I hugged my knees into my chest. He leaned forward with his elbows in his thighs.

"You haven't addressed your PTSD."

I scrunched my eyebrows, "What are you a therapist now? What do you know about what I've done? I've spent the last *five years* trying to heal from that shit."

"What I mean is," he wiped his face, "you can do all you want to overcome something, but until you face it again, you don't really know how you'll react."

"But you aren't *them*." I whispered and I thought I saw a smile slip onto his face before he stuffed it away.

"It's not about me," he said. I closed my eyes and fell back into the mattress.

"So what am I, doomed then?"

He chuckled, "I don't think so." I turned my head towards his shadow in the dark corner. He sat back in the chair, completely away from the light of the kitchen.

"You never said why you were an idiot," I said and his torso stiffened.

"I should have kept my distance." *So...he did like me?*

"Why?" I asked, because even after everything, I wanted him next to me, wrapping me into the warmth of his arms. I wanted more than a memory. I needed to feel something. Something safe, something I could trust, something like home. Not the one I had, but the one I always wanted. Something like what Ma Ingles had in Pa - wholesome and good. I never believed it could exist before. I never allowed myself to.

"Isn't it obvious?" He interrupted my thoughts and I imagined him clenching his jaw.

I flitted at Wolf's fur, "Isn't what obvious?"

"I want you, Jay, more than the air between us, I want you and resisting is like suffocating. But it needs to be when you're ready. When you're *really* ready. Not just when the desire is there, but when, and only when their touch doesn't haunt you."

I bit my lip, absorbing every word like acid and falling apart into his fluffy comforter that did little to comfort. *How could anyone be that damn wholesome?*

Tears slipped down my cheeks, "I don't know if I'll ever be rid of them. I've tried so hard for so long and the more I try to heal, the more I'm engulfed in their ghosts."

"This week isn't the best measure of that." He said.

I laughed, "Tell me about it."

"See..I told you I'm an idiot." He said. I propped up on an elbow, still unable to make out his features, reminding me of how much he'd hid as he followed me.

"On top of everything, the last thing you needed was a reminder of what intimacy has always been like for you."

"Are you saying it's something different than what I know?"

"I'm saying you deserve to feel safe," he said, repeating my own thoughts.

"I've never felt more safe than when I'm with you," I accidentally uttered out loud and he shifted in his seat.

He cleared his throat, "There's something else…I haven't been completely transparent."

"What?" I sat up all the way. My head was pulsating. What more could there be? Was this his skeleton? My stomach was turning again. The alcohol in my system forced the empty room to swirl.

"It's about your sister."

I clutched at my chest, "My what?"

CHAPTER TWENTY-EIGHT

SIX YEARS AGO

He reached into his back pocket and pulled out a folded paper before crossing the room to sit on the mattress with me. There was still so much space between us.

"Her name is Harriet," he said. I scrunched my eyes. The paper was warm when I took it from his hands. I couldn't tell what color her eyes were, though they seemed lost. Her hair was curly and white and her cheeks were the color of a dress I once wore. And so I asked the question I didn't want the answer to.

"Did they…was she…" only I couldn't utter it. Deep down I knew the answer. And when I looked up at Marshall, his brown, cavernous eyes of aching sorrow confirmed it.

I spun away and clutched at my chest. The air tasted of acid. Yellow swirled around my eyes. My parents' faces hung like ghosts before me as old memories floated to the surface. My body crawled with spiders that didn't exist, causing me to bend over.

"I …can't… breathe," I huffed. *Was Marshall saying my name?*

I wanted to destroy them. The anger inside me welled and bubbled over like magma becoming lava. *Dirty Harriet.* The name cycled through my mind on repeat. I knew that's why they named her that. I had spawned the idea. And it was because of *me*. My chest cracked as I connected the dots. Did they have her to replace me? Because I cost them all that money by running away?

There was no air to grasp. The room faded into darkness until something heavy covered my body. With my face engulfed in fur, I could only smell one thing - Wolf. I gasped and wrapped my arms around his body.

Little by little, the room came back into focus. My face felt wet and sticky. My lungs inflated with air, but when I tried to sit up, it felt like I'd just gotten off a ride at the fair. I don't know how it happened or when, but Marshall was sitting right next to me, about to reach out yet uncertain if he should.

"Jay," he whispered, "This isn't good."

"I know."

I glanced at the picture once more. Through a foggy glass in my eyes I could see her chubby, doll-like face. I screamed. Screamed at what they did…to her…to me…to everyone like us. My fists clenched into balls of ice. Wolf wrapped his body around me like a bandage as I let all the emotion tumble out. When I finally had nothing left, I swallowed a breath and leaned back from his fur to meet Marshall's gaze. Fire twisted in his eyes and a crease formed at the edge of his brow.

"What's going to happen to her?" I asked.

"She'll likely go into the foster system."

I stared at the faux wood floor. I'd heard stories about the foster system. In some cases, it wasn't much better than my own situation. In some cases, it was worse.

"But," Marshall said, "there is another option. You could adopt her."

"Me?" I questioned, my voice rattled.

"Of course, you're next of kin."

I stood up and wiped my palms on my jeans, "I don't know…"

"She'd be safe with you," his voice was soft and gentle, but it blew a raging storm through me.

"I'm not exactly a safe option," I noted as panic rose in my chest. I wanted to cry but the tears were stuck.

"Then our ideas of safe are entirely different."

"Come on, Marshall," I paced in front of the window, "You've seen me. I'm not stable. I'm an erratic mess and way too emotional to be taking care of a child."

His eyes pinned a hole into my soul from where he was still sitting on the mattress.

"She needs someone who will bat for her and protect her at all costs. I know you feel like you're falling apart right now, but you're the strength she needs. And I think you need her more than you know."

I stopped. His words tumbled around in my mind like rocks in a polisher.

"I don't even have a home," I blinked back.

Marshall pressed his interlaced fingers to his mouth, "You can stay here…until we get your van back."

I was running the thought along the fringes of my mind when Marshall stood and maundered towards me.

"But you will probably be in protective custody for a while," his finger swirled around a piece of my tangled hair. I couldn't control the shiver that followed.

"Marshall, I don't think -"

"Then don't, don't think about it now. Get some sleep, this has been a lot."

I swallowed, "Okay."

SIX YEARS AGO

The single mattress welcomed me as Marshall clicked off all the lights. Beams from the street flitted in through the window, barely blocked by the thin white curtain. Wolf nuzzled his nose into my neck and sighed. I wrapped my arms around his torso, beyond thankful to have him back.

"Goodnight," Marshall said as he settled into the wingback armchair. It looked far from comfortable. And I felt guilty. But he shushed me as I tried to protest.

"I'll be fine," he insisted, "get some rest."

But no matter how long I laid on the mattress with my eyes closed, I couldn't sleep. My mind wouldn't allow it. The room was spinning again. And my heart was feeling things it never had before.

"Marshall..." I whispered, halfway hoping not to wake him.

"Mmh...what's wrong?" his groggy voice echoed across the room.

"I can't sleep."

He shifted, "You want a benadryl?"

"You have one?" I asked.

"No."

I slapped my arms at my sides, "Then why offer it?" he shrugged and groaned out a closed lip *I don't know.* After a minute of silence I rolled to my side to face him.

"Tell me about her," I asked.

"Huh?" Marshall lifted his head.

"Your sister, I mean, if it's okay. What was she like?"

Marshall swung his leg off the arm and wiped his face.

"Allie? She was...full of life and love. I think she had more of it than the human body can hold. And her love for animals was supernatural," his voice dropped, "But when she realized the rest of the world didn't care about life, she couldn't cope."

I swallowed, "I'm sorry."

He laughed, "You know, before things got bad, she was absolutely obsessed with blue jays."

"What?" my heart stopped.

"Yeah," he chuckled, too delirious to realize I could camouflage into the ivory comforter, "She *hated* them at first because they kept eating all the paint from her flower paintings on the fence. Next thing we knew, she was feeding them eggshells because they needed calcium."

"That's …interesting," I barely uttered. My stomach was twisting up in knots. If I had any chance of falling asleep before, it was entirely gone now.

"Yeah, oh," he sat more upright, "and apparently they like to rub ants on their feathers before they eat them. Allie said it made them taste better, but I don't really know."

"Huh."

"Yeah," Marshall yawned, "that was Allie. That's why I was so caught off guard when You said your name was Jay."

"Oh. It wasn't because it wasn't Bridget?" I nervously laughed.

"Well that too," he said.

"Right. Thanks, Marshall, I think I'm finally feeling tired," I lied and faked a yawn. There was no way I could continue the conversation. I didn't even know how to wrap my mind around what he'd just said. I wiped my palms across the comforter. *She was absolutely obsessed with blue jays.* I turned away from Marshall. *What does that mean?* My thoughts raced back and forth with a hurricane of memories. Blue jays were my symbol of hope, they gave me strength to fight, to keep going, to - and I remembered Malka - to trust.

"Marshall?"

SIX YEARS AGO

"Mhmm?"

"You don't have to answer this if you don't want to, but, when did Allie die?"

There was only silence and I wondered if he even heard me.

"Almost six years ago," he finally said.

CHAPTER TWENTY-NINE

TRAPPED

A small glowing dot, like a star, entered my mind as if searching for a hidden note, a lost thing, trapped in the crevices of memory. My entire body felt like air. I almost wanted to laugh from the giddy feeling. But then tongues slid over my neck, down my shirt, and encircled every inch of my skin. My breath turned into a train engine. Darkness shrouded me. Tears streamed down my face in waves. I didn't like it here.

A melody pierced through the slithering sound, breaking apart each tongue with an arrow of light.

I opened my eyes. But I wasn't in bed. The room was dark, lit only by candle light. I recognized the room. But I'd never seen it like this before. I passed the flickering candles of cinnamon and vanilla. There was a mirror hanging over an antique dresser. The one that was handed down to me from my mother.

Staring back at me was a little girl in a purple dress. I moved my mouth and she did too. I raised my hand, but it was hers. The mirror was cold as I pressed my palm against it. Tears were in our eyes. I wished I could warn her.

The door behind me opened. It was my father. Suddenly, I was the girl behind the mirror and my reflection ran to him. My heart beat faster. I didn't want to watch, but I couldn't physically close *my eyes. I was stuck behind this damn mirror.*

"My darling," he said and kissed my forehead. He led me to the bed and I watched in horror as the memory played, reminding me of what I'd forgotten. I couldn't let it happen again. How dare he! My own father! I began to bang against the mirror. The dresser rattled, the room shook. The candles rolled onto the floor, spitting their flame into the carpet.

I screamed at him as my body shook with rage. The fire crept along the carpet and roared to a rolling torrent as it climbed up the curtains, the bed, even the walls. The floral paper of my childhood boiled and charred. I turned away, coiling inside myself. Suddenly, the heat was gone and in its place a frigid air tickled my neck. All around me was soot and embers. The ceiling had fallen in and the walls were charred with black. Wind whipped through the broken room, swirling ash in vortexes and sweeping it all away until I stood alone in the middle of a barren cement foundation. Wings fluttered from somewhere in the darkness.

I sat up in bed, panting, with my hair slicked to the sides of my face.

"Oh my God," I whispered. I had completely forgotten about that. It must have been buried somewhere deep in my mind, protecting me. Maybe this whole week pulled it to the surface. I gripped the comforter and laid back down. A lump formed in my throat. I didn't want to cry. I was tired of crying. Unlike the dream, a fire never happened. Not a literal one. That - was me.

A fervid rage had been kindled and it would not be stomped out.

CHAPTER THIRTY
THE LOOK ON THEIR FACES

The water was a smooth waterfall against my skin. Dripping and unable to see, I reached for an absent towel. Finding nothing but the t-shirt Marshall lent me, I figured that would have to suffice. My reflection was a mess. I patted and smoothed down the crazy frizz and attempted to hide the tangles. *Why didn't I pick up a brush?*

Worse than the knots in my hair were the knots in my colon. A squeamish tornado tumbled inside. I closed my eyes away from the image in front of me. *In through the nose, out through the mouth.* I repeated the mantra as I attempted to steady the drum in my chest. *I can do this.*

When I opened the door, I peeked into the backroom. Marshall lay on the floor, passed out on his stomach with his back to me. I never saw Marshall leave the chair, but I guess it wound up being more uncomfortable than the floor.

Poor guy, I thought and made my way to the kitchen. Before I'd hopped in the shower I had started a pot of coffee. And the smell engulfed me now. It took three cupboards before I finally found the mugs and I was almost afraid there would be none. I scrunched up my face at the thought and poured the coffee - only I was too busy thinking about Marshall and the black lava spilled over the cup. In my failed attempt to fumble after the mess and pressing myself against the counter, the hot coffee seeped into my shirt.

I yelped as it grazed my skin like the lick of a flame. There were no napkins or towels to be found. I bit my lip and glanced towards the hall. With a deep inhale, I ripped off my shirt and used that to soak up the coffee. I balled it in my fist and strode to the bed where the plastic bag of clothes sat. As I rifled through it for another top, something made a sound behind me. I straightened up and turned around.

Marshall was standing in the hallway by the bathroom door. His eyes were dark, narrowed at me. I wrapped my arm behind my back, as if my soiled top was more embarrassing than being topless. He wiped his mouth, failing miserably at hiding a smirk before turning into the bathroom.

I swiveled back around, feeling the heat in my face as I slipped a green thermal over my head. Thankfully my jeans weren't as affected. The bathroom door opened and I scurried back into the kitchen, letting my hair cover my face as I slipped by.

"You want any cream with that?" he asked, leaning into the fridge, causing me to cough on my drink. He shifted one eyebrow up as I choked on the fragments of liquid in my lungs. I shook my head and leaned over until the seizing stopped.

"I didn't mean it like that," he lowered his gaze as he sipped his creamer with a dash of coffee.

"I know," I said with a raspy voice.

"You gonna make it?"

"I'd rather not," I mumbled into the mug, letting the steam warm my nose. Marshall nodded. The long silence made my ears ring. So I finally broke it.

"What's the plan? And no concealing details." I commanded as I leaned against the faux marble counter. With one hand over the top of his mug, he set it down and crossed his arms.

"I'm sorry."

"I know, I just don't want any more surprises," I sighed.

"We're going to meet with a detective, a lawyer, possibly even the judge, and you can," he leaned forwards, "always decline."

I pursed my lips, "No. I want to see the look on their faces when I finally speak up."

"And your sister?" he asked.

I tapped the side of my mug. "You're right. I have no idea how anyone in their right mind will let me take her," I took a sip, "but I should try."

He smiled. It was laced with sadness and I knew he was thinking about Allie. I wanted to reach out and comfort him in some way. Though what I wanted and what I did never seemed to cross the same path.

CHAPTER THIRTY-ONE

NERVES

Marshall's knee bounced as we sat at a red light. That only made the butterflies in my stomach more furious. I didn't like meeting new people. And today I was meeting at least two. One of which was a lawyer and the thought of it made my skin crawl. I shuddered at the intrusion.

"Cold?" Marshall asked and twisted the little black knob on the dash. I nodded a smile in return.

"What are they like?" I asked.

Marshall cleared his throat, "I've never met the lawyer."

"Oh. And the detective?"

"She's...a bit rough around the edges, but has a good heart."

I clenched my lips, "I don't know how to feel about that."

"You'll be fine," he insisted. He stepped on the gas and we rolled past a red building with a black and white striped awning.

"Oh yeah," I crossed my arms, "then why are you so nervous?"

"I'm not-" but he stopped when he saw my raised eyebrow.

"Okay...I'm a little."

"Because..." Why was it like pulling teeth to get anything

out of him?

He sighed and raked his hair back, "I'm about to get my ass chewed out."

"For what?!"

"It doesn't matter."

We rounded the corner and all I could focus on was a run down two story building with a monstrous green sign reading Law Office. Not what I was expecting for a detective.

"It does matter - oh God - I think I'm gonna puke," I flapped for the handle and leaned out the door just as Marshall put it in park. But the fresh air hit my face with such force that it washed the nausea away as if it never existed.

Before I could react, the black glass door in front of us swung open and a woman with boisterous red curls came bustling out. I barely had the time to take in the deep purple pants suit before her voice tore through the space between us.

"What're ya doing? I don't have time to be waiting on you all damn day! Get inside before I shoot a hole through that bloody grin!" She yelled in a thick Scottish accent. I swung my head at Marshall, who was in fact, grinning. He didn't look nervous anymore. Must be good at hiding it.

I, for one, was not. I stood and followed him into the building behind the scott, because she wasn't about to stand around and wait on us.

"This the lass?" She asked him as we hustled past two rows of empty desks. There was a girl with long dark hair in one of them wearing platform boots; a weird contrast to the Native American decor she had around her five monitors. She gave me a bright smile as we scurried past. I awkwardly nodded in return.

"Who else would it be?" Marshall answered. The detective

snickered.

"Aye, so, here's the deal," she said as she collapsed into a swivel chair and propped her wedges on the desk. Marshall and I took the chairs in front of it as she slipped a metal flask from her breast pocket.

"Jeez, Bell." Marshall muttered and shook his head. Bell ignored the comment as she took a swig.

"We have one hour. *One.* So I hope you can keep up." Bell pinned her granny smith irises on me.

"Um, with what?" I asked but Bell didn't answer as she flipped open a silver laptop. Marshall breathed into his hands.

"Scroll until you see someone familiar." Bell swiveled the laptop to face me. Rows of mugshots glared through the screen. I bit my lip and scooted the chair in. This was going to take a while. I closed my eyes and tried to remember. But I'd been scrolling for half an hour and I hadn't recognized any one. Except for one guy. But he was a client of my parents, not the one who took me.

I rubbed my burning eyes. Marshall and Bell were both gone. They'd stepped outside the tiny office but I could just barely make out their faint voices. They didn't sound happy. I wanted to ignore it, yet my ears kept straining to hear the muffled conversation.

"Let me tell her." I was pretty sure that was Marshall. My heart tweaked as the door swung open. There was iron in my mouth from biting my lip again. A strain settled over Marshall's face as a crease formed at the very edge of his left eyebrow. The butterflies were back.

"You aren't going to like this," he started. His eyes were soft and even from here I could smell the woody scent hovering between us.

"Just rip the bandaid off," I whispered.

"The hearing is in two hours."

I reeled back in my chair. "Today?! Today? It's today?"

"Yeah."

"But don't these things take months?" I protested. I wasn't ready. Not yet. The air felt thick. The arm rest slipped under my palm as I gripped it.

"It's already been months." Bell said, leaning at the doorway. A pair of sunglasses lifted her curls from her face. She might be pretty if she wasn't mentally drilling a hole through my forehead.

"Marshall, I-"

"You don't have to do this," he said, and Bell sighed. An unexpected breeze fluttered through my hair. I shivered as I remembered the haunting dream from last night and how the dust of it all blew away. Marshall held my gaze almost as if he were holding my face in his hands again.

I shook my head with resolve. "I do, though."

CHAPTER THIRTY-TWO

NO LONGER QUIET

Either heartburn or nausea or a kamikaze combination of the two threatened to make a statement as I sat in the audience rows of the courtroom. Marshall's fingers were interlaced together on a jittery knee as mine were balled into fists, hidden away in my jacket pockets. I thought about what it might be like if Marshall were holding my hand; that maybe it would calm the raging storm inside me. *What a strange thing to find comfort in touch.* Bell's curls, tucked into a chaotic pile on her head, jiggled in front of me as she turned to us.

"How are you holding together?" she asked in a whisper as we waited for the trial to begin. I glanced at Marshall. I felt like if I said anything at all I might heave. I circled the knuckle of my thumbs. I didn't have to look at them to know they were as pale as my face.

"All rise!" shouted the bailiff. Jewelry rattled and wood squeaked as the room arose in one fluid motion. Everyone watched in silence as Judge Jones swayed into the room, her black robes swishing with an air of elegance.

A dark shadow moved in the corner of my eye, a familiar shape, sending an eerie chill up my spine. Surely it was nerves.

But when I turned my head as we were commanded to sit back down, the shadow was real. Horror shot through my body and pinned me to my seat as I took in the crooked nose, the pinhole of a chin, and the piercing of his shadowy eyes as they met mine. I might've well been hanging by one hand off a cliff, my heart was racing so fast.

Marshall's voice was low in my ear, "You okay?" he asked. Concern entangled every inch of his face as I shook my head in a visceral no. I shot my gaze back to where the man had been sitting, but he was gone. He vanished as if he was never there in the first place. I scanned the room searching for him but I couldn't find him. The doors weren't swinging as if someone had walked through. *Did I just hallucinate?* Marshall's grip in my hand brought me back and I realized that I'd been clutching him as if he were the hold in the cliff. I let go, shocked that in my panic, I'd unknowingly reached for him.

And then in bright orange, one after the other, my parents were brought in. I steadied my breath to ease the nausea. My mother, normally pristine, every perfect golden strand in order was as disheveled as my memory of her. Her left eye was swollen and the color of an eggplant. I imagined an inmate did that. My mouth went dry as I searched over my father, sunken into himself. My heart twisted as I remembered the last time I'd seen him, calling out to him. Pleading for help. I never wanted to accept that he was my enemy all these years. Even my own mind wouldn't allow it.

He was supposed to be my hero. My protector. But instead, he was the villain, and the orange fit him well - secretly, even now, much more than I wanted it to. I grit my teeth and narrowed my eyes at them. The seat was hard against my back as I straightened up.

"Calling a witness to the stand, Bridget Cummings, eldest daughter of the Cummings." I rose and took in as much air as my lungs could. My steps were pointed and purposeful. I strode with the pride of a stallion. The expressions on my parents' faces as I passed through the gate were hollow and horrified. They'd spent years, close to two decades, forcing the pill of silence down my throat. I'd been afraid of speaking, of living this moment. But I was no longer afraid.

My breath came out like molasses as I sat down in the witness seat. I stared back at them with a smile. They were getting everything they deserved. Their darkness was no longer a shroud over me. Everyone would know what they did. I wasn't holding back. My tongue was my weapon and it was poised for war.

It started slow. But little by little the words spilled out, lifted out of my body and flew away for the world to know. I watched the Jury. I saw the grimaces, the horror, the blank expressions, the nods of those who in some way were tethered to the words I was releasing, perhaps vicariously living through my openness.

I spoke about the first time - a recent memory I'd blocked for so many years. I spoke about how my mother taught me about makeup and how to do my hair and how to fix it when my tears and sweat messed it all up. Why I couldn't bring myself to even touch a simple eye shadow pallet because I was reminded of what it meant to my ten year old self.

I could barely bring myself to utter all the atrocities, but a still small voice inside told me to keep going, to let it out. Let it all go. Like wind, I blew the whistle on my parents and how they pushed me around to all their friends like a used book. How at first when I was scared, they'd even hold my hands and tell me I was doing a good job. That they were so proud.

What kid doesn't want to make their parents proud?

"Why didn't you ever say anything?" their lawyer pinned his last question on me. I pursed my lips and leaned back. Mom was staring at the wall, hollow and blank. Dad never once looked up from his cuffs.

"Because I loved them," I said. That was the truth of it. Even with everything, I still loved them and I was waiting for them to truly love me back. I realized now that was never going to happen. And as much as I wanted justice, it still hurt.

Marshall's head was bowed, staring at the floor. He knew a lot. But now he knew it all. Was he unable to see me the same? Was his anger burning? Had we not been in a court of law, I imagined he might go after my parents in the same way he'd crushed the bottle with his bare hands.

"That is all, thank you Miss Cummings," the lawyer said. I stepped down and made my way to the gate, pausing to see the horrified expressions on my parents face. Unlike everyone else, they weren't horrified at what was done to me. They were seeing someone they never knew. Someone they worked hard, tirelessly, to suppress. But you can only suppress the wild in a lioness for so long.

"Looks like you just made my day," I said and took off without looking back. When I sat down, Marshall shifted towards me. His eyes were smiling but his face was still.

"You did good," he whispered into my ear, sending a feather down my back.

"Thanks," I said. It felt as if a boulder had been rolled off of me. I might have even floated away. But something still tugged at the fringes of my mind. I'd looked when I was at the front of the room, but he wasn't here. Before I could protest, Marshall was being called up and suddenly I felt very exposed without him as my shadow.

Marshall's thorn colored eyes were pinned on me as he sat at the witness stand. The intensity of it made my heart race. And then he looked away and oxygen returned to my brain.

The lawyer I'd briefly spoken with before the hearing began kept spinning on his heels as he posed his questions. He was about as trustworthy as a shrew, but he seemed to be doing a decent job. I wondered how he would do if he was for the defendant instead. And then Marshall was done and they let him go. But something on his face changed as he made his way to me.

A scratchy voice prickled up my spine, "You."

I spun around. *What the hell?* It was his voice. But he wasn't there. Pine flitted through my senses as someone sat beside me. I turned to Marshall.

"Can we go?" I whispered. He almost answered but then they called my mother to the stand. *Was she smiling? The damn woman was smiling.* She wiggled into the seat and flipped her hair as if she were something regal to look at. I didn't hear what the lawyer asked, but I did hear the answer that caused a silent court to gasp.

"Yeah we did it, and we'd do it again and again and again. It's too bad we didn't start earlier with her." She said and flicked a bony finger my way. My dad looked about halfway to death in his seat.

I didn't react. I knew she was trying to get even in whatever way she could - if *even* meant always having the upper hand. But I wouldn't allow her the satisfaction.

"You wanna go?" Marshall whispered. *Damnit, if I go now, it'll look like she got to me.*

"No," I gritted.

He narrowed his eyes, "Okay, just say when."

I nodded with a smile. His hand slipped into mine and I swear the whole room faded away. I could have wrapped myself into him in that moment. Forget everything. But my dad's voice cut through the room and I realized I had to endure through the rest of it. By the time we got to a break for lunch, my stomach was in agony.

"Ware!" Bell called through the crowd. Marshall spun. Bell scratched her eyebrow and tipped her head.

Marshall sighed, "I'll be just a second."

"Okay," I said. I couldn't make out what they were saying, but they both looked intense. I made my way to a window and leaned against it. The sun was poking through a dark, fluffy cloud, shining a laser off the tiny drops of water hanging from grass blades. Footsteps behind me caused me to peer over my shoulder. Marshall was still in the corner with Bell.

I scanned the empty hall with the pasty white side rooms, cut out with metal chairs for sitting. A flash of movement in one of the rooms caught my attention. As I grew closer, a yellow vase slammed to the floor in the middle. It must have been plastic, because it didn't break. And then I heard him laugh.

"You're playing a dangerous game, being here, don't you think?" I called into the room. I'd just witnessed before a judge and officers about him. Why would he be here and take such a chance? There of course was no answer. Could I really be imagining him? I couldn't be. I felt fine. Better than fine. I felt better than I had ever felt.

I wasn't hallucinating. "Leave me alone!" There was no answer. No one was in there. It was completely empty.

"Jay?" A woman's voice sounded next to me. Bell of course.

"Who were you talking to?" she asked.

"Uh," I started, unsure of what to tell her, "Oh just a news reporter."

"Uh huh." she nodded in a way that said she didn't believe me.

"How are you feeling?" Marshall asked.

"Great. Just great." I smiled.

But I don't think he was buying it, "You sure?"

"I'm fine," I insisted. But then, down the hall, right at the end of the curve, he was there again. His face was twisted in rage. His blonde hair clung to his scalp, as disheveled as my mother's had been. I shoved past Bell as he disappeared around the curve. My feet ran. Harder. My breath heaved. But when I rounded the corner, again, he was…gone. Like air.

My head hurt. Darkness threatened at the edges of my vision. I grit my teeth and steadied my breath. But it was too late. I could feel it coming and I couldn't stop it. The lightness traveled through my body in a vicious wave as if I were on a ride. My body swayed. Up, down, around. The room whorled. A voice called in the distance, like a dream. My heart galloped. I tried to brace for the fall. But darkness consumed me and I fell into the eye of the storm. It was quiet there.

CHAPTER THIRTY-THREE

CONFIRMATION

Darkness gave way to golden specks flitting through a haze. Like a camera refocusing, everything twisted into a crisp image. I propped up on my elbows and blinked, trying to make sense of what had happened and where I was, but a surging ache ripped through the back of my skull.

I hissed in and reached for my head.

"Shit, did she hit her head?" Bell asked.

Marshall wrapped a hand behind me, "Don't move," he instructed. I winced when I turned to face him.

"I said don't move," he grunted as heels clicked down the hall.

"Where's she going?" I asked.

"I'd guess to find a doctor."

"Really?"

"She's not as bad as she gives off," he grinned.

I scowled, "I'll take your word for it."

"What the hell happened?" he looked pissed. Was he mad at me?

I clasped his forearm, suddenly remembering what happened. "He's here!"

"Who?!"

"Him! The guy!"

"What guy?"

"Ugh! I don't know, the guy that - man my head hurts - the guy that my parents traded me to." The clicking in the distance grew louder.

"Where'd he go?" Marshall growled with such an intensity I was almost scared.

"That way," I pointed down the hall. I doubted it would be much help now. He was gone.

"Don't move, I'm setting you down." and he lowered me. Then bolted, pausing briefly to nod at Bell. His space was taken up by a bright light blaring into my pupils. By the time the medic was done prodding me, Marshall had come back around the corner, panting.

"Well?" Bell asked.

"How is she?" Marshall ignored her, pointing the question straight at the medic hanging over me.

"She'll be fine but," and he turned to face me, "See someone about those blackouts"

I nodded and sat up, "Sure."

"He's gone, isn't he," I said.

Marshall wiped his brow, "I couldn't find him."

"That's a first," Bell shot him a look I wouldn't want directed at me. I climbed to my feet, holding my hand out to steady myself. And then quickly drew in my arm because I didn't want them to know I was dizzy.

"There! Come on!" Marshall grasped my arm and dragged me to the front door. I followed him down the steps and across the honking traffic. I contorted my face as frigid water splashed up my ankle. I'd missed that puddle. Bell watched from across the street with a glower. Her hair looked like a sunset.

"What are we doing?" I asked Marshall as he reached for the handle of a small electronics shop.

The doorbell chimed. "Hello?" A dark man with curly hair in a white linen button up asked as we charged in. He leaned back at Marshall's intensity as he towered over him.

"We have a missing child. We need to see your surveillance." He stated.

The man turned his head between us, shock crossing his face."Oh my god, yes. Back here."

"Marshall…" I whispered. *What was he talking about?*

"Hurry up." Marshall grit his teeth as the man led us into a back room. He was completely ignoring me!

The curly haired man flitted a glance at us. "Just a second."

He clicked away at a mouse, rewinding the black and white video. It showed the sidewalk in front of the building and the entire front of the courthouse. We watched as people carelessly went about their day with smiles plastered on their faces. They seemed so oblivious.

"There. That's us." Marshall flicked at the screen.

I strained my eyes "I didn't see him."

And then, there he was behind us, confirming my sanity.

CONFIRMATION

I held the print out picture in my hand. It felt like a million shards of glass pressing into my fingers, surely the worst kind of paper cut. My feet sunk into the hard navy carpet.

"Do you trust me?" Marshall's words seared through the warmth of the shop.

"That's not exactly a comforting question," I responded. He pushed his eyebrows together.

"This isn't going to be easy, but I have an idea," he sighed, "but it won't work if you don't trust me."

"What, Marshall, what's your idea?"

"Jay, please," he begged. I rubbed my hairline and glanced around the room. The world was gray outside the window, and I saw no signs of life. Could I trust him? I found the brown depths of his eyes pinned on me. I opened my mouth to speak but nothing came out. I bit my lip and prayed for a sign. Just a little one. But there were no feathers, flapping of wings, or the sweet call of a jay bird. I had no sign. Could I really trust whatever plan he had?

"Okay." I said

"Okay?"

I nodded and held my breath. I had to take a leap if I wanted to be free. Maybe I'd fly like a bird - or I'd fall...like a bear. Marshall nodded us away from the ears of the shopkeeper and lowered his voice. His eyes were intense and his lips taught.

"When we leave here, we'll meet back up with Bell. She's going to give you a tracking device."

"A tracking device?!" I spit in a whisper, "You're gonna use me as bait?!"

"Yes," he stated without blinking. The room felt thick with humidity.

"Mar-"

"We can end this, Jay, all of it. Not just this guy lurking around you. But the entire thing. The whole trafficking ring. No one else has to be hurt by them anymore."

I sucked in a breath and held up my hand, "Wait, so we're not talking about just him? Like, you capture him, question him, torture him for info? You want me…to lead you…into the whole damn hive?" my voice went up an octave and the shopkeeper spun his head on us.

Marshall walked away, ran his hands through his hair and turned back. "You're right, it's too much. I'm sorry. Just forget it." I could see he meant it. There was sorrow in those eyes. He wanted to destroy every last one of them. And he almost put me at risk to do it. And yet, his words were ringing true. Maybe we could end it all. Maybe I didn't have to live my life constantly looking over my shoulders. And maybe it wasn't just about me.

I lived my whole life thinking I was the only one. *No one knows what it feels like to be me.* But there *were* others. Others that knew every ounce of pain I endured. And they were trapped right now in a life I was able to escape. What if it were me in there? What if it were Allie? Or Harriet? I glanced up at Marshall with a glaze over my eyes and a deep fear striking my heart.

"I'll do it."

CHAPTER THIRTY-FOUR

A LEAP OF FAITH

The warmth of my pockets enveloped my hands. The tracking device, though smaller than a pendant, felt as heavy as an anchor. I could still feel Detective Bell's fingers on my skin where she secured it in the privacy of the women's bathroom. A place where, hopefully, those dark eyes wouldn't catch onto what we were about to do.

"What about the rest of the trial?" I asked as I smoothed my shirt back over my torso.

"You're not required to be there," she stated.

"But what about you or Marshall if you're needed for questioning," I asked, still terrified of something going awry with the plan.

"Stop worrying your knickers off," she scolded. "Everything's gonna be fine."

I nodded as Bell pulled the thin black strap of her purse over her head.

"Besides," she said, "Imani owes me. I got her brother his dream job."

"Imani?" I asked.

"Judge Jones."

"Oh."

"That and Scotland's finest liquor," she mumbled and I tried to fathom the story behind that statement.

"Ready?" she asked, hand hovering above the handle.

I sighed, "not really."

"Let's get them," she pulled down her sunglasses and opened the door. The fresh air hit me in the face like a punch. I couldn't believe I was actually doing this. The one thing I tried to avoid the last five years I was now facing head on. And for the first time in my life, I wished I wasn't alone. I remembered the tracking device. *Hopefully not alone for long.*

"Catch you later!" Bell called as I made my way back to the green sedan where Marshall waited. Only… I wasn't going to make it there and Bell's words felt like an ominous hint.

The air pricked at my nose, insisting I turn back and run away from this ridiculous plan. I clenched my jaw and kept my head down. I twirled the blue necklace hanging over my clavicle for some kind of comfort. But my legs still shook as I peddled down the damp sidewalk. My heart pelted against my ribcage. And even though I knew it was coming, the sudden grasping of my body, yanking me into the alleyway, forced a scream through my trembling lips. It was him. His eyes narrowed on me before clasping a hand over my mouth.

Before I could attempt to fight him off, a thin sharp pain penetrated my neck. The feeling in my hands and feet flooded towards my heart. The man grinned and a chill rushed down my back. He didn't try to contain me. He didn't need to. And before everything turned to nothing, he bent over and whispered in my ear.

"You're not getting away this time."

I tried to open my eyes, but the darkness wouldn't go away. When I tried to reach for my face, I felt a pull at my wrists. They were tied behind my back with what felt like very rough rope laced with some kind of chemical, burning through my skin. That's when I realized there was something tied around my eyes. But my mouth was free.

"Hello?" I pipped. It felt asinine calling out like that and I almost rolled my eyes at myself. There was no answer. Only the hum of something familiar. I couldn't quite make it out. A distant thrum of metal rolling, like a heartbeat. A hand clenched my arm and I reeled back into a cold wall. A gurgle of a laugh pointed at me.

Then light pierced my eyes as the blindfold fell away. I winced until my sight adjusted. A flash of a shadow flew in my peripheral before a searing pound smashed into my face, throwing me back against the wall again. My vision went blurry as my entire head vibrated with the throb of a thousand pounds. I could feel something warm dribble down my lips.

As I assumed, it was the blonde haired asshole from before. He was sitting on a stack of luggages sipping a Pepsi. His face seemed to be carved of stone, like some Roman hero of old. Pride flicked through his eyes, matching the almost flawless features of his profile. What would have been flawless if I hadn't broken it in. If I didn't know who he was and what he did, I might almost mistake him for a model. I could imagine how many young girls fawned over his handsome appearance - but I wanted to hurl. He was too pretty, too smug, and far too full of himself.

Pale gray squares flashed by in the window. I knew exactly where I was. An underground coffin. Of all places, he had me on a train. A funny tingle swirled in the pit of my stomach as he leered at me. If I stretched out my leg, I could probably reach his boot. I was staring at the leather when something flicked my forehead and bounced to the metal floor.

It must have been horror that stretched across my face as I stared at the crumpled tracking device, because blondie was far too happy.

"What? Are you sad now? Your boyfriend can't find you, oh you poor thing," he mocked with a laugh. I grit my teeth and went to lunge, but stopped. Suddenly, I could care less about the man in front of me. My legs weren't working. No matter how hard I concentrated, they wouldn't budge.

"Told you, you weren't getting away."

"What did you do?" I whispered.

"Don't be so freaked out, it's only temporary," he shrugged. "You're gonna need your legs for what they're doing with you."

I took a sharp inhale, "Who?"

He smiled with a lean and pinched my cheek, "Wouldn't you love to know."

It took everything in me to not spit in his face or turn my head and bite his hand. A screech and a huff and the train slowed to a stop.

"This is us. Get up - OH! Wait! You can't." He teased with menace and hoisted me into an upright position. There was no one in the cargo, but there had to be someone at the station. He was going to have to untie me.

"Shit." I muttered, now face to face with his chest. I didn't know how I missed it before. He was decked out in police gear. No one would question anything. But he couldn't keep me from yelling...

Only when we stepped out into the flickering green subway, not a single person was there. It felt too surreal, like some parallel universe, or a bad nightmare. Graffiti swirled over sheen tile walls. The train inched its way down the tunnel and blondie continued to grip me to his side since I couldn't use my legs on my own.

Midway down a flight of stairs, an elderly woman hobbled past us. She didn't look our way. And I didn't say anything. I was afraid he might hurt her if I did.

"You're gonna go far kid," he whispered in my ear and dropped me. Maybe it was a good thing I didn't have my legs. I'd love to kick his nose in again. He took something long and charcoal in color from the side of his cargo pants and began prying at the tile.

With a crack, a panel came loose, opening to a small dark hole.

"Get in," he ordered as he hoisted me up.

"No." I resisted, panic pricking the entire surface of my skin. Not like I could get in by myself, he was going to have to move me. He grunted and shoved me through the narrow opening, my feet dragging along the concrete before I was falling to the ground again. It must have been the worst feeling in all my life. I wasn't just trapped by my own mind. I couldn't run away - literally. There was nothing I could do.

We were shrouded in darkness as he stepped through and

shut the panel behind us. It didn't take long for him to click on a flashlight. But it was still too dark for me to make out what sort of place we were in. It felt much larger than it should. As he hoisted me over his shoulder, the swish of fabric seemed to echo across a canyon.

Blood rushed to my head and nausea swirled in my stomach. I was acutely aware of exactly where his hand was holding me. I bit my lip to keep from lurching away, certain he'd drop me again - but this was much higher up. I was thankful he wasn't as tall as Marshall. My heart swirled thinking of him, hoping he was as good of a tracker as he said he was. I hoped he hadn't lost me without the tracking device. Now all I had to lean on was one person. I had to trust that he knew what he was doing. But as we went farther into the depth of this mysterious shadow, I feared I was about to be lost forever. No one would find me here.

The turning of a handle echoed into the silence, and a narrow light flooded out from the open door. It was hard to tell, but I swear it looked like a mall food court from the eighties.

I pinched my eyes shut as the brightness of the new room enveloped me. And then I was chucked to the ground again. This one had carpet, though it wasn't much to soften the landing. I clenched my jaw to keep from yelling out at the jolt of pain reverberating through my side.

"Thank you. Your portion. If you'll wait here, we have another assignment for you." a new melodic voice said.

"Will do," blondie replied. I still didn't know his name.

"Now, Miss Bridget...or is it Jay?" he hummed. I opened my eyes. The carpet was a dull mahogany and the walls a dirty shade of white. The man in front of me didn't look threatening. In fact, he seemed about as normal as anyone else. His hair was gray and his slack pants were camel. The watch on his wrist looked older than me.

"Yes, I know all about you, Jay. And what you've been up to in the last five years," he said and my stomach turned, sweat beaded at my hairline. *Was the room closing in?* I wondered as the walls seemed to tilt.

"Such resilience. That goes far to swoon people. And swoon you will," he beamed.

"Swooning isn't hard when all they want is my body," I glowered and his hand twirled a piece of my blonde hair.

"What do you think, Jordan, actress or singer?" he squinted his gray eyes at me.

Jordan grunted, "I don't give a shit."

"What are you talking about?" I questioned.

"You'll find out soon. Men?" he said and backed away as four men came into the room, surrounding us in a circle. They all looked identical with bullet proof vests and AR-15s. I scooted back, *were they there the whole time, lurking in the dark?* The one in the middle right reached for me but I socked his knee. He buckled forward and I swung my elbow into his groin, eliciting a groan. Two of the others grabbed each of my arms and lifted me into a stand.

Jordan smiled and waved. I'm sure he was happy to see them overpower me. I pushed my shoulders against their restraint but I couldn't break loose. Then I smiled back though my stomach swirled in knots.

"You *will* pay for this," I swore. He rolled his eyes and turned away from me as the gray haired man handed him what looked like a usb drive. I couldn't see much more because the armed men were yanking me back through the door. We fell into darkness. My eyes adjusted to the area I was being pulled through as my feet dragged across marbled tiles. The air was stale and tiny orbs of dust twisted through the vast space.

A chill slithered up my back as I took in all the shadowed stores like little individual black holes. Some had their gates down. Most didn't. By the smell of it, I imagined an invisible wall of mildew crawling across the side of what was once a store called Afterthoughts. This was a mall…underground, empty and abandoned. And the men were dragging me deeper into it.

My stomach rolled into my heart as we approached an escalator. One side was dead, the other - the one going down was running. I couldn't help the trembling that started in my hands. It was almost pitch black at the bottom of those escalators, but my eyes had adjusted enough to make out shadows inside one of the stores. Perhaps it was ironic that the store was the name of a well known children's brand. I'd been in one as a child, but it looked nothing like it did now.

"What's down there?" I asked as a set of eyes locked on me and sent my heart racing.

But I didn't get an answer.

"Go," one of them flicked his gun at me as another started to drag me onto the moving escalator.

A tingle radiated through my legs. I pushed against them with everything I had, but my floppy limbs were no match against the men. My fingers scratched at the end of my sleeves as I opened and closed my shaking hands.

The men nudged me along. I grasped onto the railing, afraid that if I went down that escalator, I'd never come back up. Or if I did, I wouldn't be the same. Shadows expanded to the outer edges of my vision until I gave in and squeezed my eyes shut.

Please God, rescue me. I couldn't go into whatever this new kind of hell was. Malka and her family were so certain of their faith, so certain of a loving God. I needed that God right then, I needed someone to love me enough. I needed someone to save me from this, because I couldn't do it on my own. I gave everything I had, but my strength had disintegrated into dust. I wasn't going to escape this time.

As if answering my plea, a gentle breeze waved over the top of my skin and wrapped around my entire body with warmth and comfort that whispered into my ear and elicited a shiver through me. It enveloped around the erratic beating of my heart before fluttering out through my hair like a gentle caress. A familiar whistle echoed from above. In the ceiling, perched on the head of a humpback whale hanging from metal chains, was a little blue jay.

"How'd that get in here?" one of the men muttered.

CHAPTER THIRTY-FIVE
FREE

A blur of a shadow flashed before me, pummeling into the men. The gloved hands ripped away from my arms, causing me to slam face first into the cold tile floor as a loud shot ruptured through the mall. Glass shattered. A scream echoed below as someone fell to his death.

A section of the pony wall behind me that separated the first floor from the second was now gone. I tried to get up as boots scuffled in front of me. Broken shards of wall were everywhere. Each move was met with a sharp stab.

As soon as I got to my feet, I was falling again, knocked back by Jordan rushing past. I tried to grab for anything as my body fell through the hole. He paused. There was fear in his eyes. I just barely caught a metal piece, fragments of glass slicing into my palms. Jordan gathered himself and took off as my arms clung at the ledge, my legs now hanging over the second story floor.

But there was no grip in the tile.

Years of rock climbing had never prepared me for a precipice like this. My fingers and shoulders burned as I reached forward. My abs seized up. And as I grit my teeth and pulled my body forward, I swore I heard disembodied wails from below. A surge of adrenaline thrusted my hips to the side and I was free from falling.

I clutched at my heaving chest and finally looked up at the madness transpiring around me. Marshall, clearly noticeable by his fluffy brown hair, was pounding fist after fist into one of the men's ribs. Two of the others lay unconscious on the floor. A storm of rage made every muscle in his face taught as he grabbed one of them by his collar and slammed his nose into a neon orange metal chair. Blood splattered into the air, sprinkling like crimson rain over Marshall's forearms.

Light was still flooding out from the open door, but there was no one inside that room.

"Marshall," I called out, "There's more here, but I don't see them." I said as he wiped his hands on his black cargo pants. He dressed similar to the men, decked out in a tactical uniform. There was an automatic pistol on each leg and a rifle strapped around his back.

"I know," Marshall picked up one of the AR-15s and tossed it to me. I gripped onto it like a life-source as Marshall made his way to me, unclicking his vest.

"What are you doing?" my eyes blinked at the rate of my heart.

He pulled the vest over me, "Not letting you die."

"But what about you?!"

"I'll be fine," he said with a wink and lifted me to my feet. I wobbled as the entire length of my legs to my toes tingled until they felt like they were being stabbed a million times over.

"I hate liars," I mumbled before an echo of something crashing to the floor caused us both to glance across the open chasm to the first floor. Jordan was making his way for the hole in the wall. He was going to escape. I'd be damned if

I let that happen. I raised the gun Marshall had thrust into my hands and clicked back on the trigger before my thoughts could convince me otherwise. And Marshall - he didn't stop me.

It was dark and hard to see, but Jordan fell to the ground. I'd hit him. He, at least, would never hurt anyone again. But as I went to make my way over and assure his death, Marshall's hand pulled me back.

"Cover your ears," he wrapped his arms around me and spun us 180 degrees, clutching me into himself like he was some kind of shield. My ears ruptured as the wall by the train station exploded. My heart jolted and I screamed.

Building debris flew in every direction, breaking both glass and drywall. The heat of a fire could be felt near the explosion. Dust encapsulated us. I found myself clutching onto Marshall as what I could only imagine was a SWAT team storming through the rubble.

Under it all was Jordan's corpse. There was no surviving that.

"Get her out of here!" Marshall yelled to one of the men charging our way.

"Come on Lass, you heard him," Bell said as she wrapped her arm through mine. *Woman charging our way.* Her hair, though pinned up, was like a torch.

"Wait, what are you doing?!" I yelled at Marshall. Surely he wasn't staying behind.

He pulled the butt of his weapon into his shoulder, "I need to see this through…you know I do. Now go!"

Before I could protest any further, I was being yanked away by a very strong Scot. One of the SWAT men, who had already made it down the escalator, yelled up to us.

"You'll never believe what's down here," he said. But I couldn't make out the rest as Bell pulled my stumbling self through the rubble and back out into the train station. I held my shirt over my nose, coughing through the dust. As we reached the top step and rounded the corner, gunfire could be heard in the distance. I clutched at the gun Marshall gave me, holding my breath and offering a prayer that he was okay.

I'd spent so many years by myself, not wanting anything to do with anyone. I even thought I might die happy alone. But now, I had someone to care about and I wasn't sure I could handle a world without him.

Bell must have seen the worry stretched across my face as we began climbing another set of stairs to the surface.

"I won't promise you that everything's gonna be okay. But he is a good marksman, one of the best, and if anyone has a chance of making it back, it's him."

I eyed her sideways. I could still feel the healing wound on my hip. I didn't have her same confidence - even if I did just watch him take out three armed men single-handedly. As I wobbled up the last step, gray light piercing my pupils, I thought about how Wolf and I were somehow minimally injured from that accidental gunshot.

Maybe...

But as I waited in the passenger side of Bell's black sedan, and men in uniform swarmed around the subway entrance, I couldn't calm the shaking in my hands.

Wolf's head rested against my lap, the only sure thing in the whole world at that moment. I had to remove his collar so he quit smacking my face with it. My legs no longer tingled as I repositioned myself in the seat.

An orange glow fell over the metallic city as the sun set.

Human shapes emerged from the dark tunnel under the sidewalk and I bolted up, my hand hovering on the door handle. As their faces came into focus, it seemed as if they weren't mentally there, staring into some far off place. There were men and women of all ages and while I couldn't put my thumb on it, I could swear some of them seemed familiar.

And then I saw him. And I was out of the car, running through the crowd. My heart wanted to burst. Wind whipped through my hair as I weaved through the throng of broken souls. And then I reached him, breathless and barely able to keep my sobs contained. His face was red, doused in evidence of death. And his eyes - his beautiful brown eyes were glazed over, haunted in a memory.

"It's done," he whispered, "You're free."

CHAPTER THIRTY-SIX

HOME

The building loomed in front of me like Everest. The sun reflected off black glass doors and while I didn't need a jacket, I found myself rubbing my arms to erase the chill. *I can do this.*

Marshall opened one of the doors, standing on the side as I passed through. I glanced at his face, remembering the blood spatter on him from yesterday. *It's done. You're free.* And I knew it to be true. There would always be evil in this world. Danger would continue to lurk around every corner, and my memories may always haunt me, but something in me healed knowing that my parents were locked up and the men after me were dead. Marshall was supposed to restrain them, take them into custody. That was the plan - but the plan went sideways and I suspected - I hoped - that after seeing the endless cages of abused people locked away underground, they knew the responsible party deserved a fate more gruesome than a cell.

They didn't deserve to continue breathing. Even if there were worse things in life than death. While part of me wanted an eye for an eye, to make them feel what they've done, the right thing was just to end it all. And maybe, just maybe, I could heal enough to move on and really start living. Figure out who

I am and what it is I like without my mother's influence or demands.

I swallowed as I glanced at Marshall, realizing for the first time why he kept asking me about my favorite things.

Before I could tear up, two men in uniform and a conveyor belt greeted us. I clenched my fists and reminded myself that they weren't going to hurt me.

"Empty your pockets, ma'am," the one said. I bit my lip as I rifled through my jeans. There wasn't much there. I made sure I left my gun behind.

Marshall followed suit like a robot preset knowing the drill. As I waited for him to gather his wallet and keys, I kept fiddling with my hair. My head felt naked without my beanie, but it didn't seem right to meet a judge with it. I already didn't have the greatest attire.

"This way," Marshall pointed down an empty corridor with fluorescent yellow lights and no windows. The sound of our steps echoed off brown tile. We turned the corner into a small waiting room with white flowers. It smelled of fresh paint. I tried to focus on the smell so I didn't focus on how anxious I was.

"You're gonna be fine," Marshall whispered. I laughed and flitted with my hairline. His eyes were like melted chocolate. I wanted to lay my head against his chest and hear the beating of his heart. In it, I might hear mine too. But I resisted the urge and twiddled with the hem of my sleeve.

"I never did ask," he said, "but what ever happened to you after I left for help?"

I smiled, "A jewish family took me in. One of them was a doctor."

Marshall winced, "I am sorry. That got way out of hand. I

should have never allowed it to escalate like that - I should have-"

"I know a lot about should have's," I interrupted.

"Still..."

"You know, Bell says you're a great shot and I have to wonder how on earth you managed to shoot us and barely create an injury."

"Luck. I'm a shit shot and Bell knows it."

I thought about that and about the bear, and the blue jay, and what I'd felt back in that mall.

"I don't think it was luck," I stated. He raised his eyebrows. God and I...we weren't on such bad terms anymore. I don't know why my childhood had to be robbed in such a violent way, but someone's been looking out for me these last five years - making a path in the wilderness. A way where there was none. *Was it God? An angel? Allie?*

"Bridget Cummings." A female voice echoed and I winced. I really hated that name. I stood and Marshall was next to me in an instant. The woman smiled at us, causing two little dimples to dip into her cheeks.

"Just Miss Cummings, sir." She said in a voice that belonged to a chipmunk. I glanced at him, nervous to be by myself again. He nodded at the woman.

"I mean it, Jay," he said and somehow I believed him. I followed the heel clicking woman as her ponytail swished back and forth. Marshall's eyes were on my back, watching like lasers as I disappeared into another room.

This one, though it had sunlight, was much darker. There were full bookshelves on every wall except the one with the window. In front of the window was a long mahogany desk and behind it sat an older woman speckled with the darkened dust of a sun. She peered at me over the metal rim of her glasses.

"Please sit," she motioned to one of the chairs in front of her.

"Yes, ma'am," I said. The nameplate on her desk read Judge Imani Jones. I smiled at the ring of it, and of what Bell had said.

"First off, I see you've had a name change, is that correct?"

"Yes," I responded.

"And you go by Jay Vanda now?"

"Yes."

"Very good," her voice was silk as she flipped through a folder of papers on her desk. Every time she tipped her head forward, a bit of light would bounce off the metal pen holder and stab me in the eyes.

"Tell me about yourself," she said as she clasped her hands over the pile of papers. I wondered what was there. What kind of information she had.

"What do you want to know?" I asked as I rubbed my forearm.

She smiled, "What have you been up to in the last five years?"

I bit the corner of my upper lip, "Uh, well. I went to Montana. I was homeless the first year but I did whatever job I could find. Usually without pay. And someone took notice and gave me a job that paid. I stayed at a homeless shelter until I had enough for a van. And then I started living out of my van and taught myself how to edit videos and then the last year and a half I've been living out of my van with my dog as a freelance editor." My gaze went from the corner of her desk where I was staring, back up to her face. Her chin rested over her fingers.

"I have your tax records here. Honey, you've built yourself from the ground up haven't you?"

"I guess I did," I said, chills tickling the back of my neck.

"The question is," she said, "Can you care for a child?"

I wiped a strand of hair out of my eyes, "I think so."

"No," She shook her head, "This is not a thinking matter. You better well know and you have a minute to convince me."

The sigh that came out of me felt as heavy as stone. I didn't know how to take care of a child. When girls my age were babysitting, I was an adult play toy. I didn't even have siblings…until now. What did I know about raising children? All I ever cared for was Wolf. But that wasn't the same. And if I was completely honest, he was the one taking care of me.

"I've been alone for a long time. I've never been able to trust people having grown up with my parents. So I don't expect you to trust me. I don't know if I would even pick myself for her. But I know she needs someone who cares, who will protect her, and who will be there when she asks why her parents aren't. I don't want her to be hurt again."

The judge leaned back in her chair without a word as she rubbed the rim of her gold cat eye glasses. She swiveled in her chair to look out the window. I felt like passing out, holding my breath for so long.

"Here's what we are going to do," she said, swiveling back around and letting her glasses hang around her neck, "We are going to give you custody,"

My body remembered to breathe again and my eyes went wide. The judge held up her hand.

"On a preliminary basis. That means, from time to time, a social worker will be checking in on you."

"Yes, ma'am." I said, excitement rising…until I remembered I didn't have my van and had essentially no place to live.

"Well, Miss Jay," her dark cheeks rose, glimmering with

speckles of gold, "You may go back to the lobby and your sister will be brought out."

"Okay...thank you!" I said and tried not to jump too fast from my seat.

"One more thing," she said. I turned around with my hand almost on the handle.

"You take care."

"Yes, ma'am."

"I mean that now. Second chances don't come often."

I nodded with a smile. How many nice people could I meet in one week? Maybe I was making up for a lifetime of only knowing evil. But evil was often wrapped up in a pretty bow. I'd like to believe for just once that wasn't the case for everyone. And as I walked into the waiting room, seeing Marshall lift up his head, and his puppy dog eyes inspect my face for a tell, I knew I'd found someone good. Not the fake kind. Not the ones that are as lovely as almond blossoms on the outside but inwardly were a walking graveyard, eager for souls.

"Well?" he asked, standing as he held onto his jacket. I realized this was the first time he wasn't in long sleeves. Veins laced his forearms in a way that made my knees weak.

I bit my lip, holding in the tears, "They gave me custody. On a preliminary basis." His smile was like a blue sky.

"See, it's all going to work out." He said it so confidently. And the punch of reality crashed into me. I had no home. I had to take care of a child. I couldn't do this. The room began to fade to black and my feet felt numb. *Oh God, I'm going to pass out.*

"I can't," I breathed, shaking my head.

"Yes. You. Can." Marshall smelled of mint. I squeezed my eyes shut, dug my nails into my palm and let the tears fall.

When I opened them again, Marshall wasn't holding onto his jacket. He looked tense, like he was about to catch me. Feeling crept back into my feet and the darkness faded.

"You don't have to go this alone," he whispered, his hands open, reaching out in question to me. An invite. I blinked and wiped away the tears, stopping midway across my face. At the very edge of his sleeve were paint speckles of teal and navy. I tilted my head, staring, trying to focus on what I was seeing.

In a millisecond, Marshall shifted and I knew. I'd seen it so many times, that even just the very edge, the tiniest tip was all I needed to see. It was the tattooed tail of a blue jay, in watercolor.

I ignored Marshall's hands. I completely fell into his body, wrapping my arms around the back of his neck. At first he was stiff and then he melted into me. His arms enclosed around my back, pressing me into him like a weighted blanket. And for the first time in forever, my breath felt even. Every ounce of fear dissipated. I was okay.

I was okay.

Our foreheads met, our breath heaving in ragged unison. This is what home was always supposed to feel like. I tilted my head and pressed my lips into his, hot like fire, but soft as a rose petal. My heart exploded into every cell of my body and I pressed deeper into the safety of his arms. His hand caressed the side of my face, sending shivers down my arms. And then he broke away to stare into my eyes. And without saying a word, I felt the entirety of a love I never knew could exist.

A woman's voice echoed my name in the distance. I let go of Marshall, letting my fingers fall slowly along his arms. He squeezed my hands and nodded. *This was it.* When I turned around, there was a woman with a jet black bob and at her side, a little girl, golden curls spilling over her tiny face. She was wearing faded overalls and a white shirt with little pink flowers. Fear flowed in her eyes.

My sister.

I knelt down and she leaned into the woman as she clasped her thumb into her mouth. Her eyes were like the sky, almost as striking as Wolf's.

"Hi," I said. She stared back and I waited. Then she let go of the woman's hands and made a mini step towards me. She blinked, uncertainty flitting over her face. I smiled as warm as I ever had.

A small smirk dashed on her face for a brief moment before she made another step. I scooted closer and so did she.

"Hi, Harriet. I'm your sister," I whispered, barely believing the words I was speaking. With a thumb still in her mouth, she raised her free hand. It fell softly against my cheek. I closed my eyes, the warmth of her palm on my face was like the sun on a cold day.

Then in the same moment, we both took a deep breath.

Resources

If you or someone you know has been affected by sexual abuse or trafficking, please know you are not alone and there is help available.

The National Human Trafficking Hotline is a national anti-trafficking hotline and resource center serving victims and survivors of human trafficking and the anti-trafficking community in the United States. The toll-free hotline is available to answer calls from anywhere in the country, 24 hours a day, 7 days a week, every day of the year in more than 200 languages. **1-888-373-7888 TTY: 711 Text* 233733**

Stop it Now! provides free, confidential, and direct support and information to individuals with questions or concerns about child sexual abuse. Anyone concerned about child sexual abuse can reach out to the national prevention Helpline **(1.888.PREVENT)**, email, and chat services, an interactive Online Help Center, and the "Ask Now!" advice column." Helpline call hours: *Monday 12pm-8pm EST; Tuesday 12pm-6pm EST; Wednesday 12pm-6pm EST; Thursday 10am-6pm EST; Friday 12pm-6pm EST.*

Victims/Survivors | Human Trafficking | Office for Victims of Crime (ojp.gov) All victims of human trafficking deserve to feel safe and supported. Quality care, compassionate responses, and essential services can help victims recover from their victimization. OVC has compiled a list of resources to help victims and survivors receive the assistance they need.

Child Victims and Witnesses Support Materials for Victims of Human Trafficking, Office for Victims of Crime, January 2022 For children and youth, participating in the justice system as a victim or witness can be especially confusing, distressing, and even re-traumatizing. Child Victims and Witnesses Support Materials was created to support children and youth during their involvement with the justice system as a victim or witness to a crime. Based on the input of national experts and lived experience experts, these materials are intended to teach children about how the justice system works, what their rights are, the roles of the different practitioners they'll meet, and how they can cope with the difficult feelings they might have.

FIND SOMEONE LOCAL - https://humantraffickinghotline.org/en/find-local-services

INSTAGRAM ACCOUNTS

Polaris Project

Our Rescue

Exodus Cry

The following resources are intended for adults who have experienced childhood sexual abuse and are seeking support.

aftersilence.org

1in6.org

locator.apa.org

https://thearmyofsurvivors.org/

bravemovement.org

hiddenwatercircle.org

thelamplighters.org

malesurvivor.org/

https://nomoredirectory.org/

www.rainn.org/recovering-sexual-violence

https://www.road-to-recovery.org

https://www.snapnetwork.org/about

https://saprea.org

survivorschat.com

stopitnow.org

timetotell.org

Acknowledgments

First and foremost I must thank my Creator and God, who without, I'd be nothing. It is because of Him that I am here today and because of Him that I have a love for people and stories. From Him came both the ability and deep desire to write. I only hope I can honor Him in the gift He has given me.

Next I want to thank my mom and dad who both purchased the equipment I'm using to write on instead of the broken and slow laptop I was tapping away at. A core memory of mine is my mom reading to me as a child as I lay against her chest. And some of my fondest moments were of her taking me and my sisters to the library. We may not have always had much, but we never lacked books. Both my mom and dad have been huge supporters of my writing and have listened when I've yapped about my stories. Every writer needs someone who will gladly listen to their ideas.

Next I want to thank my sister Roni, who is like the most amazing person ever. Who has taken two jobs to financially support me and my two girls when I lost my job and wants me to pursue a career as an author.

Next I have to give a massive shout out and thank you to the team of people who made this book possible. To my beta readers and critique partners, I truly owe so much. To Jasmine, Shania, Susan, Alysson, Ali, Brandi, Rebekah, and

Caitlin. I also want to thank my editor Alysha Thornton - I know you only did a sample edit because I wound up being too broke to hire an editor for this book, but you still deserve the recognition and I can't wait to hire you for my future books.

Thank you to Abbie Emmons, who doesn't know me, but her words "your story matters," kept me going when doubt started to creep in.

Thank you to my high school journalism teacher for tricking me into journalism where I first found my love for writing and revision.

Lastly, I owe the world to Chad. I would not be writing again if not for you. If you hadn't insisted that I was an amazing writer, if you hadn't pushed me to enter that short story contest, if you hadn't been overwhelmed with emotion from reading that short story - I wouldn't be an author. You beat yourself up all the time because you want to give us the world, you want to do so much for us - but you have. *You have.* I'm living my dream because of you. I owe you everything.

About the Author

Mare is a mother of two girls in North Alabama. When not writing, you can find her homeschooling, cleaning house, baking, reading, praying, failing at gardening, laughing, hyperfixating on a random craft, rollerskating, dancing to oldies, playing ping-pong, watching video games and quoting movie lines.

You can connect with me on:
- https://mareephrathah.wordpress.com
- https://www.threads.net/@mare.ephrathah.writes
- https://www.instagram.com/mare.ephrathah.writes
- https://www.youtube.com/@MareEphrathah

Subscribe to my newsletter:
- https://bit.ly/mare-author-newsletter

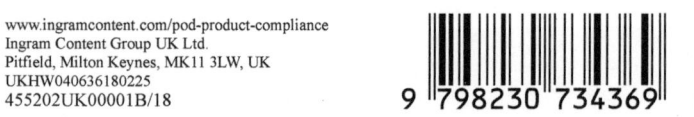